A GENTLEMAN DETECTIVE AND OTHER WESTERN STORIES

RICHARD PROSCH
with a foreword by John D. Nesbitt

THORNDIKE PRESS
A part of Gale, a Cengage Company

T0243418

Copyright © 2023 by Richard Prosch.
Thorndike Press, a part of Gale, a Cengage Company.

Thorndike Press® Large Print Softcover Western.
The text of this Large Print edition is unabridged.
Set in 16 pt. Plantin.

LIBRARY OF CONGRESS CIP DATA ON FILE.
CATALOGUING IN PUBLICATION FOR THIS BOOK
IS AVAILABLE FROM THE LIBRARY OF CONGRESS.

ISBN-13: 979-8-88579-019-2 (softcover alk. paper)

Published in 2023 by arrangement with Richard Prosch.

For Wyatt

A GENTLEMAN DETECTIVE AND OTHER WESTERN STORIES

TABLE OF CONTENTS

FOREWORD

BY JOHN D. NESBITT

The western short story does not have much to define or limit it because it has such a wide-open range of potential. It is the American short story or the modern short story, as one may choose to describe the short story in general, with its only restriction being in the setting. This may not seem like a big item until one compares the western short story with the western novel. The traditional western novel is a novel first, but in order for it to be a western, it has to have a western setting in time and place, and it needs to meet some expectations of the genre. It has to have a clear conflict, and the conflict has to have a clear resolution or determinate ending. Even if a western writer does not want to write cookie-cutter westerns, to some extent the work will be read, responded to, and reviewed as a western. The short story, in contrast, has more freedom — not only in topic, method, style, and tone, but in shape or form.

Some people, even some western writers, have limited notions about western short stories. I have heard and read some authors declare that a short story is like the first chapter of a novel, that it is a practice ground for writers who will go on to write the real thing (a novel), or that it does the same as a novel but on a smaller scale. While these generalities may be true of some writers, they are not true of writers who have a fuller command of the craft.

Whenever a writer goes back to the board or back to the well to start a new story, all possibilities are open. Good short story writers try not to write the same story twice. They try not to duplicate stories they have read. Reading interviews of writers helps us understand how stories work. One common question for interviewers is where an author finds ideas or develops ideas for stories. Writers have many different answers, as different stories come into being in different ways. Most of the time, good stories do not come from a single source in story line or character or idea, as the author reaches inward and draws at will on the best material in that huge reservoir.

Although the world of short fiction is open

to great variety, short story writers face some small-minded obstacles. Some readers have fixed expectations of what a story should contain. For example, some readers expect every short story to have a reversal or a twist. Some readers expect every western story to be resolved by a gunfight or a fistfight. And most curious of all, some readers complain and give low ratings because a short story is not long. What the author hopes for, and does not always get, is an open set of expectations on the part of a reader.

This is the third collection of stories I have read by Richard Prosch (the previous two were *Devils Nest* and *One Against a Gun Horde*), and the stories herein are new and original. As I read the individual selections in *A Gentleman Detective and Other Western Stories,* I was reminded of other western short story authors such as Emerson Hough, Max Brand, Bennett Foster, Ernest Haycox, Alan LeMay, and Bret Harte, as well as traditional writers such as Ambrose Bierce and Ray Bradbury, and, for a moment, Richard Brautigan. But those are just my impressions. My broader inference is that Richard Prosch has developed his craft by reading a wide range of greater- and lesser-known practitioners and that he has drawn from a wide experience of western life and human character.

I hope that the reader comes to each of these stories with the idea that here is a new story and let's see how it works. No two stories are alike, and there is much to enjoy in this collection.

John D. Nesbitt is the author of more than thirty western novels and more than ten collections of short and mid-length fiction. He has won the Western Writers of America Spur Award for Best Short Story and the Western Fictioneers Peacemaker Award for Best Short Fiction.

THE VIEW AFTER SUNSET

The Sonny Wagner place sat up there in Dakota territory on a prominent hill, sort of a bluff really. Under a wash of endless blue sky, it was the perfect place for a barn. There were no real trees to speak of then, and the open range to the northwest let the wind rip through every day, all day long. Sonny and his wife, Rose, wanted the gambrel roof barn to set close to their two-story frame house in hopes it would cut the wind blowing in from the north by half — which was nice if you were working on the roof, where I was.

I shivered as I looked down into the scrub-grass yard where Sonny's plans finally came to fruition.

The old boy had taken forever setting stakes for the barn, piddling on it here and there, digging footings, procuring rocks, sand, and cement.

He was dead now, but at least his barn

would soon be finished.

Some of us had been over before, when Sonny was still kickin', helping him with laying bricks, shoring up the foundation, raising walls.

Making progress sure . . . but slow.

Just like the cancer that ate Sonny up in August.

Us men figured we owed it to Sonny's memory to complete the crooked thing before the first snow.

Crooked, that is, to my way of reckoning.

But Bill Mullins yelled up at me, "Not so, Gil. Everything here's as straight as Noah's ark."

"I guess you'd know," I called back.

Bill was a big deal Mason from a long line of the brotherhood. Always keeping things on an even keel, our Bill. Always with the balanced eye.

Sandy hair like mine, better teeth, tall and leathery. Folks on the bluff said me and Bill Mullins could pass for brothers.

I didn't have a real brother and kinda liked being an only child.

But Bill was okay. Solid — if not as square as folks would have believed.

Just like Sonny's barn.

Bill hollered up again, "Gil MacDonald,

you wanna come down and see for yourself?"

I waved him off and almost lost my damn balance.

Tell you what — take a tumble off Sonny Wagner's barn, and you'd remember it for the rest of your life. What there was of it.

Forty by forty square and sixty feet high with a double-pitched shingled roof, the barn had four half-X doors, a handful of glass windows, and was topped with the ornate weather vane I'd just finished nailing down. For all my complaints, the thing was practically a work of art.

From down below, Donnie Moore gave me a smile and a quick wave indicating his approval.

Donnie had brought the weather vane's iron horse to life in his smithy's forge with coal fire and a steel hammer. "Goodest vane I ever built," he said. "Looks real good!"

Donnie was my brother-in-law. Full of muscles like chunks of cordwood (and that's just between the ears) but with the surprisingly gentle touch of an artist. He wasn't much for words, but he could finesse the hell out of a stream of white-hot metal whether it was for horseshoes or dainty wedding rings.

And Sonny Wagner's cousin little Sam

15

Willats provided the barn's apple-red paint. "Visible for miles around."

We all had a hand in the supply chain long before we gathered at the job site.

Before he passed on, Sonny had most of the lumber cut and ten bags of square nails squirrelled away. The oldest of our five-man crew, Tom Potter, snow-white and balding, wanted the barn pegged together with wood dowels, but Sonny head been more forward looking. He wanted to use the nails.

"We're doing this for Sonny," I had said to Tom. "For his memory. We ought to do it how he wanted it."

"We'll use the nails," said Tom. But he wasn't happy about it.

Even with the newfangled square nails, the barn rose up and held together. It didn't have much choice with us five owlhoots pounding and sweating, measuring, sawing and lugging. We lashed the walls and rafters together. Tight! We secured the windows and doors, fast.

It had been an ambitious project for the five of us — let alone for one man on his own to attempt.

By first frost, with Sonny gone, nobody was gonna let the Wagner barn sit half-done through winter.

Like I say, we had a hand in the thing already.

At first, the widow Rose turned down our help, but I said, "Call it an anniversary gift." She would've been married to Sonny twenty-five years that November 10, 1885.

"It's the least we can do," said Bill. And saying so, we had a deadline.

Mason Bill, and Thick Donnie, me and Sam Willats the painter, and old Tom, we had less than a week to finish the job before the red-letter day.

Thank the Lord for the Wagners' home-grown sawmill. Sonny's machine ran off a Clark & Howard knockoff steamer, and once the boiler got cooking — watch out! The thing made a hell of a racket, and the engine valves were leaky, but the shavings smelled clean and fresh. We didn't have so much to cut anyway, because Sonny had prepared some before he passed.

Old Tom and Bill Jordan ran the saw while Sam and Donnie hammered away.

We tried to divide the work up even.

Thick Donnie was our Samson. The man can hold a framing stud like a pillar. Little Sam's a master joiner, and Bill the Mason kept the whole thing plumb — or so he says.

I sorta supervised the outfit, hurrying around back and forth between them, figuring out what needed to happen next and generally keeping the peace between the crew when the men knocked heads with one another.

"I think Gil's getting the best end of this deal," Tom said.

We worked sunup to sundown and into the dark of night and sore muscles.

And we did it again the next day. And the next.

By Thursday morning we thought we had it licked, but a scattering of black clouds started piling up on the horizon. Before we knew it, big dollops of rain pelted us like spit-wads from heaven. And the rain came with ice.

Just an irritable damn nuisance until finally one of them clouds cut loose for real.

About that same time, the smell of onions and bacon and fried chicken came drifting in from the house. It was Rosie putting together our midday meal.

The new weather vane secured on top of the barn, I carefully made my way to the tall wood ladder leaned up against the side of the barn. As windy as it was, I was glad to be off the roof and back on solid ground. With the rain coming, we all worked inside.

Donnie's trusses held rock solid against the wind — with nary a rafter creak, thanks to Mason Tom. No drips thanks to the tidy shingles Sam and I had laid down on the roof.

We wheeled the heavy back door shut on the big rollers Mason Bill installed, and the crew kept at it, finishing up the inside and anticipating dinner. We worked together, breathing in the smell of freshly sawed lumber and humming along with the hard slap of the downpour outside — me and Bill and Tom and Donnie and Sam.

It was a good feeling. Nobody called our work *charity.*

Eventually, I looked at my pocket watch, and when both hands hit square on twelve, I suggested we break off for chow.

It was Bill who first said what all of us were thinking.

"With the wet weather setting in, we may not have the final lick of exterior paint dry by tomorrow night."

The Wagner's anniversary.

Old Tom rubbed his knee and said, "This one feels like it might keep to raining all weekend."

"It's a darned shame," said Donnie.

We all felt the same way, knowing it didn't matter if the final touches weren't done precisely on time to celebrate Rosie's anniversary.

But still we moped.

Retiring to the dining room, the realization had us in low spirits, especially little Sam who'd been hoping to slap his red paint around once more, an exercise now unlikely with the deluge.

Rosie said grace. A clap of thunder came at the *amen.*

We talked about Sonny as we passed around the bowls of buttery mashed potatoes, fried apples and onions, green beans with bacon, fresh bread and churned butter. It was Rose who started it.

"I can only imagine his face," she said. "If only he could see the magnificent work you all have done for us."

Old Tom crossed himself and so did Sam, and we all agreed Sonny could see us from his lofty position on high. It was us who had to imagine his gratitude.

"You've done more than anybody could've asked," said Rose with a sigh. Then, as a new layer of gray clouds darkened the room, she delivered the blow we already felt. "It's a shame you couldn't have finished by tomorrow night."

She wouldn't have had to say it, but she did.

With the rain spatter against the plate

glass windows, we all muttered in agreement.

We weren't going to make it.

The barn wouldn't be finished for the wedding anniversary supper after all. Not with the naked walls and the rain coming down.

I watched Sam nibble at his biscuits and jelly, itchy with nervous energy, but nowhere to go with his brushes lingering outside in cans of kerosene.

I realized Mason Bill was quiet for a change, his voice directed inward as he contemplated his chicken wing.

Tom and Donnie washed down their taters with water, and the room dropped in temperature. I guess the iron stove in the corner was cooling down after a morning's hard work.

In the end, it was Bill who spoke up first. As always.

"Are you sure there's nothing else we can do for you, Rosie?" He rolled his thumbs around. "If there's something else we could do . . . ?"

He let his words trail off, which was unlike him, but we were all feeling the strain.

It wasn't like our crew to miss a deadline, and even if it wasn't our fault, we each knew it was.

We could've worked harder, faster.

We could've started sooner.

Or prayed harder for fair weather.

We felt we needed to make up for it somehow.

Rosie was all too keen to oblige. "There is a small job up in the southeast bedroom ceiling. The heavy rain's got me to thinking about it."

Tom said, "You got a leak needs fixed?"

"We do. Sonny never got to it, and . . . well, I'm afraid it's ruining the wallpaper, and . . ."

"Say no more," I told her. I put both hands flat on either side of my empty plate and pushed up and away from the table. "Let's go take a look, boys."

As one, we rose up from our dinner and trundled toward the stairway. "I reckon I've got plaster at home," Bill said.

Sam chimed in, "And I can mix up some tar if need be."

Rosie sent her blessings up the stairs behind us. "It's the room on the left," she said.

Turning into the room, expecting to find a leaky roof, the first thing all of us saw was the painting.

Before Bill could worry about plaster, or Sam, the tar. Before Donnie or I examined the wrinkled wallpaper or Tom could poke at the brown ceiling stain . . . we lined up in front of the tall easel and its rendered landscape.

"Will ya look at that," I said.

Nobody had to tell us what to do. We couldn't peel away our attention.

"No wonder he piddled around on the barn, taking so long to get anything done," Bill said.

Because Sonny had been busy upstairs.

The room we gathered in was a gallery of natural oil paint landscapes. More than a dozen paintings were nailed to the walls around us, and each was signed "Sonny Wagner." Windswept trees with autumn leaves. Cows grazing with contentment. A dog dozing on the household stoop.

Just as sure as Sonny had stocked up on lumber and bags of nails for the barn, he'd gathered provisions for his paint room. A fat shelf leaned floor to ceiling against the north wall, its shelves crowded with little glass jars of pigment. Dozens of brushes, sponges, and palette knives were visible, and Donnie almost tripped over a bucket of kerosene.

"I hope Sonny didn't light his pipe up here," said Sam.

The fumes were pretty strong.

"It's the sunset view from the top of the bluff," Tom said.

I turned my attention back to the stretched canvas before us — surely Sonny's masterpiece. Four feet by four feet, the natural outdoor scene was immediately familiar to me. The valley I'd just been surveying from the roof of the barn.

But more impressive.

Somehow Sonny had managed to capture the cold clarity of the indigo sky with its first sprinkling of stars better than Mother Nature herself. He'd sparked the crimson fires and amber reflections of the horizon. He'd sketched in the burnt umber grass and the ocher and forest green cedars.

"What a swell choice of color," Sam said. Being the expert on such things.

"But it ain't done," Donnie said. He pointed at the lower left and right of the plane. "Here, and over here. This part's unfinished."

Bill agreed. "The trees have no leaves. The pond has no reflection."

There was no two ways about it. "Sonny died before he could finish it," I said.

Tom nodded. "Just like the barn."

We all put out a heavy sigh and looked past the easel to a three-legged table where a round painter's palette was smeared with

24

a crazy mess of drying paint. A handful of brushes lay scattered there and on the floor. A couple jars half full of colored kerosene and a pile of rags sat on the floor.

"This horizon is out of plumb with the edge of the canvas," said Mason Bill.

"Since when do you know art?" I said.

"Dammit, Gil, just look at it."

I squeezed my eyelids and peered at the scene. "Aw, I think the smell of the place is getting to you."

"Here, give me one of them brushes."

Before anybody could move, Bill had a brush and was swishing it around in a jar of kerosene. While we watched, he dabbed the brush into a sticky pile of brown palette paint and drew a long, horizontal stroke across the middle of the picture.

Then he stood back and cupped his chin in hand.

"Better," he mumbled.

"He's right, Gil," Tom said.

"He usually is."

Donnie put a forefinger to his nose. "For my way of thinkin' though, the yellow in the sunset is wrong."

I nodded, wondering if Donnie imagined the fire in his forge at home. "You've got a point."

"Gimme that brush," said Donnie.

Tom handed over the tool and Donnie dabbled around with some dry orange without much success. "Anybody see any fresh paint?"

"There's a little jar of red here. And some gold." Sam handed it over. "You mix up some orange and let me in on it too."

The two men conspired on the color, mixing gobs of pigment directly on the canvas while I stood back and directed. Just like with the barn, I played supervisor.

"A little more red over here on the right. A touch of yellow to the left," I said.

"Say," said old Tom, "I think that much fire would show in the pond's reflection." While he talked, he picked up a brush and loaded it up with a booger of turquoise. Then he smeared it over the face of the water.

"That's good," I said. "Keep it coming."

Tom continued to smear the paint around, adding some blue from a crusty glass jar before instinctively picking up a brownish red tone. "That's almost a magenta," he said.

"Alizarin crimson," Sam said, knowing his paint.

"A lizard what?"

"Never mind."

I laughed and asked Bill to straighten up

the cedars in the foreground.

Now all four men worked on the painting, the canvas just big enough to accommodate the communal effort.

With a brush in each right hand, the quartet of workers were like musicians, each with their own special instrument, each layering their individual sounds one over the other to create a symphonic master-piece.

"Pick a color for the foreground grass," I told Sam, but he was already ahead of me. "Tighten up the canvas up top, Don."

"I need a straight edge," said Bill. "Any-body got a straight edge?"

I looked around, found a spare broom handle propped up in a corner of the room under the leaky wallpaper. "Here you go," I said.

Bill laid the broom flat on the surface and traced three vertical lines. "Pine trees," he explained, then nodded out the window to the open range where a trio of sprigs danced in the wind. "Bigger than life," I said, and he gave me a wink.

"Straight as Noah's ark."

I put the broom handle back in the corner.

"We might need an ark if this rain keeps up," said Tom. He stood and rubbed out a brush with a clean rag he found on a top shelf.

From somewhere in the old ceiling above, a drop of water tumbled down and splashed my nose. "You'll just have to wait your turn," I said.

I figured we could fix the leak in the ceiling later.

As things were, we had more pressing work.

"We've got an anniversary painting to finish," I said.

"It's what Sonny would've wanted," agreed the crew, and we set back to work.

Step by step, stroke by brushstroke, the sunset view came into focus.

Tom finished up his waterscape, and Donnie added horizontal, pink clouds at the horizon, trailing long and wormy above the prairie.

Bill got his evergreens lined up, and Sam finished up the grassy foreground.

I decided the sky was too barren, and with it being harvest time, we ought to add a bright pumpkin moon.

Surprise — Bill agreed with me. It was Tom who drug his feet on that one, concerned about how it would look with the reflection he'd already established on the surface of the pond. Donnie came to the rescue with his orange paint.

While we squabbled over the moon and Sam cleaned some brushes, a part of me couldn't help but wonder what Sonny would think if he saw us.

What a scene the five of us must've made in front of the sunset.

What a view Sonny had, from the other side.

Five old neighbors, handling dainty brushes, bickering about shades of pigment like ladies in a dress shop, tripping over our calloused fingers and leather boots to finish a good work.

It just goes to show how much we never knew about Sonny. Picturing him in my mind, I thought about his big belly, his beefy wet laugh, his robust head of curly gray hair and long muttonchops.

He was tough-skinned and red-faced. He had bad teeth and was a mean drunk. He and Rose never had kids.

I never knew him to pet a dog or raise a kitten.

Yet there was a side to him on display here, in the secret upstairs of his home. Not a dirty secret. Nothing ugly or rotten. But a sweet side, a gentle side. Something if I thought about too much, I'd get red-faced and embarrassed with.

It just goes to show you.

Then I felt like we had almost gone too far. Like we'd intruded on Sonny's private space enough. Maybe Sam felt the same way. He was the first to call it quits for the day.

"We ought to stop and let her dry a little."

"I wouldn't mind seeing a patch of wild-flowers down here in the corner," Tom said.

"Add 'em tomorrow when the grass is dry," Sam said.

Bill said. "We'll finish the sky up too. Add a few more stars."

"I think it looks good as it is," I said.

Donnie: "You think we need a circle around the moon, Gil?"

I shook my head. "Too busy."

"Yeah."

"Yep."

"Uh-huh."

We all agreed.

Tom wiped his hands and put down his rag. "Just thinking — this room probably gets good light in the morning."

"I'll bet Sonny did his painting 'fore noon," I said.

"You want, I'll come back over and do up them flowers after I get done feeding cows in the morning."

Not to be left out of the loop, Bill said, "I

could touch up those trees a jag."

"I'll be here if you are," said Donnie. "Sam?"

The little painter seemed to catch my expression from the corner of his eye. "I don't know, fellas. I think I might be busy in the morning."

Looking around the room, looking at each other, we all started to shuffle our feet.

"I guess I've got my own harvest to get to," said Tom.

"Ought to maybe get over and fix that leak in the ceiling though," said Bill.

Again, the sense of intrusion.

We had almost overstayed our welcome. It was time to retreat.

Before we left, Bill stopped us. And for maybe the first time in his life, he asked my honest opinion.

"Gil . . . uh, you think we ought to . . . uh . . . sign Sonny's name 'fore we leave? Sign the painting, I mean?"

"I think he'd be honored if you would, Bill," I said.

Bill having the steadiest hand.

We all lowered our heads to wait, listening to the rain on the roof overhead, fidgeting now, with itchy feet ready to leave as Bill made a flawless copy of Sonny's signature in the lower corner.

"Happy anniversary, friend," he whispered.

And we all hurried off down the stairs as fast as we could to where Rosie had coffee brewing.

Like little boys guilty of doing something improper.

WAKING FACE

Ever since his wife was murdered, Deputy Sheriff Martin Greer couldn't sleep. Four months had come and gone, the seasons changing from spring to summer, the interminable days stretching out longer, the brief respite of night shrinking fast.

Mary had been the first to die under the blade of the unknown killer's midnight knife blade, but she wasn't the last.

After the most recent killing, Sheriff Dodd Carter called his deputy in to the office, but the weight Greer carried was nearly suffocating.

Once more, he felt waves of nausea and a pounding headache.

Once more, he was racked with guilt.

Because, to the best of anyone's knowledge, Deputy Martin Greer was the only man to have laid eyes on the killer.

But Deputy Martin Greer couldn't describe him. He couldn't remember the killer's face.

He dawdled on his way up Main Street.

Shuffling through the dust of Holt City, he stalled.

Across from the sheriff's office, Greer passed the tall, wooden Indian prominent on the boards outside Miller's Tobacconist shop. "Howdy, Chief," he said, and walked inside, his heavy boots echoing on the floor.

The place smelled fresh and clean with scents of lemon wood oil and rich Virginia leaves.

The tobacconist sat behind the counter whittling on a piece of cherry wood. " 'Morning, Greer."

"How do, Seth."

"What'cha need?"

"Bag o' Maple Jack. For the pipe." Greer didn't smoke a pipe. He was planning to start.

"Big bag or little bag?"

The question caught him off guard. Miller peeled a slice of wood away from a block of cherry in a fat, slow rolling curl, until it fell joining the others on the floor. The morning sun glinted on the edge of his knife.

"A little bag, I suppose." Then: "You're awful good with that blade."

Miller tossed his work to the counter, stood up, and dusted his hands, seemingly embarrassed. "Not so good."

"Who taught you?"

"Nobody. I'm what you call self-educated. First thing I did was the chief out there. But it took me so long, I switched to birds. Ain't no big thing. I've never gotten too proficient."

Greer didn't let it go. He reached over the counter and picked up the whittling. "Looks like a songbird?"

Miller filled a small canvas bag from a glass jar full of rich, loamy tobacco. "Supposed to be a blue jay."

Greer studied the piece. An artist by trade, he'd painted portraits for rich folks in Denver because he made them all look better than they really did. After that, he'd been handpicked by the governor to accompany General Wilkes's expedition to South Pass and render the frontier in charcoal, pen, and ink. Once he married Mary and settled down, his editorial cartoons sometimes ended up in the weekly *Holt City Times*.

Greer was an artist with an eye for detail.

"It's fine work."

"Means a lot, coming from an artist with your talent, Deputy."

Greer laid down the wood and dug in his pocket for a coin.

Miller handed over the sack. "No charge."

"Are you sure?"

"Go ahead. Hell, we all know what you've been going through with Mary. Least I can do is share a good smoke."

Here it was again. The sympathy Greer found heaped upon him.

His anger in response. The impotence Greer felt whenever he thought about Mary.

Whenever anybody brought up her murder.

The deputy's throat swelled, and his eyes burned. He tossed his coin to the counter. Gritting his teeth, he said, "Don't bother with the charity. I'll pay my way."

Jamming the tobacco into his coat's side pocket, he left the store without bothering to pull the door closed behind him.

The fresh June air made the inside of the shop suddenly seem stuffy and sickly sweet with the smells of so many different tobaccos.

Greer snuffed hard and pulled himself together.

Beside him on the porch, Chief Virginian stood lifeless with his arm in a warlike posture, his right arm high, tomahawk in hand. Waiting to attack.

Greer said, "Wish I could trade places with you, Chief." Staring eternally into the morning sun, the heavy pine carving remained unmoved by Greer's words.

Greer pursed his lips and set a new course for Sheriff Carter's office, hardening his heart.

"I wish I didn't have to feel anything."

He waited for a teamster to speed past in a tall-wheeled wagon, and a fancy dude in a long duster rode past on a silver mare.

The kind Mary rode.

Before.

Greer slowed his pace. The sheriff's office loomed in front of him.

He didn't want to hear about another killing.

If only he could sleep, he thought as he slumped in a chair across the desk from Sheriff Carter.

"Another knife through the lungs," Carter said. "Just like Mary. Just like the Hamilton woman, and the Rogers girl after that."

It was like Greer's ears were covered in cotton batting, and he asked his boss to repeat every other sentence. "Another church social, wasn't there?"

Carter was sympathetic, but Greer could tell the sheriff's patience was wearing as thin as a circuit preacher's first pair of shoes. "You know it as well as I do. You were at the Presbyterian picnic yourself."

"Sure," Greer said. "Just lining up the

details in my mind."

The picnic was the fourth such Sunday event in Holt City since Easter. Each gathering setting the stage for another taking of an innocent young life. Carter and Greer hadn't made the connection between a church social in the afternoon and a murder at midnight until killing number three, sixteen-year-old Emma Rogers of the Congregational church.

As far as Greer knew, nobody else had seen the pattern.

But they would.

Before long, everybody would realize it. Especially if there was another murder.

Greer said, "Catholics are having some kind of beer garden thing in a couple weeks. You think we should have them postpone it? For the time being, all things considered?"

"You go ahead and tell Father Mac he's not getting his beer on St. Agnes What's-her-name-day. See how far that gets you." Carter put both hands flat on his desk. "Oh, no. Not me."

"It's been rough for you too. I know it."

"The town is getting impatient with us. I've had at least a dozen men threaten to string me up these last ninety days," Carter said.

"You're doing the best you can."

Carter brushed off the remark. "We damn well better get a handle on this thing, Martin, and we better do it soon."

Greer rubbed his temples, was nursing another headache. Everything about the case was a dead end.

And his own witness to the initial crime was the deadest lead of them all.

Carter came around the desk, perched on the edge to address him with the informal posture of a friend.

He said, "You still can't remember the face?"

"No."

"And still not sleeping?"

Greer shrugged. "Ten minutes here, twenty there. I dozed for almost an hour the night before last."

"How much sleep do you think you're getting each night? How much all together?"

"No more than three hours. Maybe four, spread out over a span twice as long."

"Have you tried a stiff shot of whiskey?"

"Shot, tumbler. Bottle. If it worked, I'd be in dreamland every night."

"And you could tell us what we want to know."

"Tell you," Greer nodded. "I could draw him for you." His pencil renderings of suspects and known lawbreakers graced dozens of pasteboards and wanted posters all over the region. "I'm sure I've seen him before, but . . ."

It was so damned frustrating.

"Go home," said the sheriff. "Try not to think about it for a while. One of these nights it will come to you, and we'll wrap this thing up."

Greer was skeptical but held his tongue.

Stranger things had happened.

Things like his beautiful young wife of only three years being viciously knifed through the lungs in their bed.

Things like Mary left to drown in her own gurgling blood as Greer leapt up in the dark of a curtained room. He had lunged through the bedroom door behind the killer, stumbling over his own discarded trousers. He'd called on the man to stop, damned himself for not having pulled his gun from the corner post of the bed.

It had all happened so fast — the break-in, the intruder striding into his and Mary's room.

The killing blow.

At the kitchen window, the killer had turned so his entire face was awash with moonlight, and Greer immediately recognized him as someone he knew. A familiar visage — but the name balanced on the edge of his tongue, refusing to fall. "Stop, damn you," he had yelled again, charging forward, reaching out, only to fall once more, face-first into the cabin's hardwood floor.

Scrambling up, he followed the intruder outside, but it had been too late. Greer had caught only one last, fleeting vision of his quarry darting between two cedar trees back toward the direction of town.

But then he heard the death whimper of his beloved wife from behind him, inside the house.

And by then it was too late.

That last mournful cry wiped out everything, including the man's face.

A face Greer knew, and could draw . . . if he could only remember.

A face that even now he was only able to glimpse in part while sleeping. A waking face he could only glimpse in that limbo between slumber and daytime awareness.

And more often than not, he couldn't sleep at all.

That Thursday night Greer stayed up past midnight, playing with his pipe, experimenting with the tobacco Seth Miller supplied. Pipe smoking was a damn sight more complicated than he'd reckoned on. Tamping

41

the leaves, pulling in the fire, puffing, puffing, trying to keep the damn thing lit. Trying not to choke on the smoke.

He used up three bowls of Maple Jack before he got the hang of it, and by then he was queasy and light-headed. He walked outside his lonely cabin and sat on the doorstep while moon-fired clouds passed above the high prairie horizon, blotting out the eastern stars.

As always, he thought about Mary. How much she had enjoyed that last day. That last afternoon at the Lutheran church's family day. There had been cake and cookies, lemonade and flour-sack races.

Mary had come to the gathering with her banana bread and ginger cookies. The old men in their shirtsleeves and suspenders, lounging around the fishpond puffing on their cigars, and Seth Miller, smoking too. And the sheriff with his plug of chewing leaf.

Was the killer present that day? Was he there, someplace in the crowd?

Greer strained to recall — impulsive, clumsy.

Like reaching for a jumping frog, he tried to grasp the elusive mental image of the killer, and it slipped away. A hummingbird, ducking, darting out of reach, it hovered just outside his perception.

Greer fell asleep, and the faceless killer taunted him in dreams.

Mocking, evasive, shrouded in maple-flavored smoke.

Brandishing a knife.

In his dreams, the face appeared full in sunlight and Greer wrapped his hands around the neck just below the chin holding on for all he was worth.

Upon awakening, it was gone.

The charcoal stick stained his fingers brown and left a trail of fine crumbles on the hard-woven tooth of the pulpy paper.

By lantern light, drenched in a thin film of sweat, he worked it out.

Hunched at his kitchen table, back muscles and shoulders quivering under the labor, he worked the media, left and right. Up and down. Subtle shades.

Soft thin lines receding into the paper plane, a trick of perspective.

Heavy lines advancing to form a cleft chin, the circumference of a high, flat forehead.

Greer pieced the image together, line by line, rubbing out each draft with the palm of his hand. Smearing the charcoal. Tearing the paper.

It wasn't about talent.

It was about labor. Pure and simple. Muscled memory and years of practice. Knowledge of anatomy and how the elements of portraiture worked together.

He clipped the chin, rounded the ears.

Smoothed out the carved geometric bags under the dark eyes, rubbed away the overemphasized eyebrows.

Greer's heart raced as he followed one road, abandoned another. His quarry was there, just ahead.

He almost had him.

Then he brushed away the tall, phony Indian headdress, added a close-cropped thatch of stiff, thistle hair.

"I've got you now, Chief. I've finally got you."

Except for fits and starts, Greer hadn't slept soundly for weeks. When he finally recognized the killer's face as that of Chief Virginian, the wooden Indian standing outside Seth Miller's shop, he couldn't remember feeling more wide awake.

A chortle came up like involuntary bile, but it didn't sound exactly sane.

Rolling up the final portrait, Greer was roused by a sense of justice.

More, he was energized with vengeance.

Friday morning, Deputy Sheriff Martin

Greer marched through Main Street with a purpose. In forty-eight hours, the Catholics would be putting on a spread in Holt City park and fiddlers would weave tunes around the tables of ham and beans and cornbread, cookies, cherry cobblers, and peach pies. The sheriff would be there, and the doc, and all the merchants from downtown. Father Mac and the Methodist minister and the Congregationalist preacher would be there too.

The entire town always turned out for the beer garden. The young women would be adorned in their finest.

Greer was determined they would all survive to see the next morning.

He took two steps onto the boardwalk, gazed at the wooden Indian there, then kicked in Seth Miller's door.

Startled by the noisy upset to his morning routine, the tobacconist slid off his seat to stand at full attention behind the counter. He dropped his knife on the counter with a bang.

"M-morning, Greer."

Greer wasn't feeling charitable. In fact, he felt downright mean.

Slapping down his tube of drawing paper, unrolling the portrait he'd drawn, he made one demand. "Who is he?"

45

Miller was compelled to answer fast. He was shaken. Stuttering.

"He's o-out front, Deputy. You know that. Y-you just passed him. You pass him every day when you come in."

"Not the statue. The man."

Miller swallowed hard. Scared.

Greer reined in his anger, struggled with his righteous enthusiasm. He spoke slow, holding back with each word, trying desperately not to pick up Miller by the shirt collar and shake him into a mound of putty.

"Who is he? Who's the man you modeled him after?"

"No model. I just . . . I just carved a face. You know I ain't so proficient."

Now Greer did grab hold of Miller. The man was limp, breaking out in sweat. Like a wet dishrag.

"I swear to you, Deputy."

"I'm tempted to believe you, but the thing is, Miller . . . I've seen him. Seen him walking through the moonlight in my kitchen." Greer put a growl into his voice, still doing his best to hold back. "Last time I checked, the chief out there doesn't have any feet to walk."

Greer let Miller go and the shopkeeper bumped into his chair and wiped his forehead, smoothing back his wild bangs of hair.

"You oughtn't be so rough. There's no need to be."

Greer's attention was drawn to the black-handled whittling knife on the counter. Amidst a clutter of shavings, the blue jay was developing well.

Greer said, "You're good with a knife, ain't you?"

Miller's expression went from anxiety to outright panic.

"I ain't had nothing to do with them dead girls, Greer. I swear to you. I had no reason to hurt Mary or any of them. You know that, don't you?" He seemed to shrink into himself and his voice rose an octave. "I'm your friend."

"Yeah." Greer's stomach rolled, and a hot, rancid taste rose in the back of his throat. "If you mean it, you'll answer my question. One more time. Where'd you get the chief's face?" He rattled the paper portrait on the counter. "Who's this man?"

Miller's defense was battered and gone. All he could do was answer. "He's my brother, Jonah."

"Where is he?"

"You need to understand. He's not right in the head."

Greer roared. "Where the hell is he?"

"At my place. Out west of town. In the

47

potato cellar. I . . . I keep him chained there during the day." Miller laced his fingers together. "He's not your man, Greer. I swear, he can't be. I watch him all the time."

"What about when you sleep?"

"I don't understand."

"Who watches him when you sleep?"

"He's locked up. I swear."

"You're sure of it? Because I think when you're asleep, Jonah is awake. And he's at work killing women."

When he left, Greer pushed the wooden Indian over with a crash, snapping Chief Virginian's tomahawk arm off at the shoulder. "Sorry, Chief, it's not your fault."

Greer kicked himself for not realizing early on the wood carving shared the face of Mary's killer. It was the problem of context. Like seeing your schoolteacher out of place at the mercantile store. Or catching the preacher at the saloon dressed in work clothes.

Greer went straight to the sheriff's office, walked inside. Carter was out, his desk, empty.

After leaving a note, Greer took a key from the center desk drawer and walked to the gun rack. He unlocked the middle security board and took down his favorite lever-action Henry.

Along with the tied-down holster and its Colt single-action Army revolver on his hip, the rifle ought to give him the advantage over a man who worked with knives.

A stinking skunk whose victims were defenseless young women.

Greer left town on a red roan, all alone, with the wooden face of Seth Miller's brother leading him on to the claim west of Holt City.

The sun was still low in the east.

He'd arrive at his destination before noon and, once he did what had to be done, devote the weekend to slumber.

The sleep of the righteous.

After a while, it wore on him.

Riding on the river trail, the long-stemmed prairie grass rolled away from him in waves on the wind, and he held tight to his hat with one hand, the reins of the roan with the other. His fingers still bore the smudges of his morning art. He carried Jonah's portrait with him, stuffed into the leather rifle boot next to the Henry.

Greer wasn't going to risk losing the face again.

As he rode, the vast panorama of wide open country diluted his anger, leaving only sadness in its wake. The backwash of righteous indignation was bitter sorrow.

Far off to the west, the mountains were a wash of indigo footed with interwoven strands of gold and green. Above, the stormy sky was rich with blends of powder blue and thick cobalt.

He felt the muscles in his neck relax. His eyelids droop.

"Aaaaaaaa!"

The scream descended toward him like the predatory call of an eagle. Greer's eyes flew open to a single pinewood talon swinging toward his chest.

The impact of Chief Virginian's tomahawk arm, swung like a baseball bat from the back of a careening black horse, flung him from the saddle onto the ground.

Greer landed on his tailbone, hitting the hardpan with a crack. He rolled to his side, desperate for the butt of his gun.

Spooked by the sudden assault, Greer's roan whipsawed away in the opposite direction with the rifle in its boot.

The attacking horse and rider wheeled around and came thundering back down the trail to take another turn. Greer fought the pain in his lower back, levered himself up into a crouch, and drew his Peacemaker.

He fired up into the air.

The slug caught Seth Miller in the shoulder, but not high enough to be superficial. A patch of red blossomed on his shirt, faster than life would allow.

He slid from his saddle, crashing to the ground only a few feet away.

Greer stood over him with a twitchy trigger finger. "Don't try anything," he said.

But even as he said it, he felt foolish. Miller's fight, and life, was soon leaked out onto the sod.

The deputy shoved his gun back into his holster and reclaimed his horse. His back was sore, and his ribs ached from where Miller clubbed him with the hunk of pine.

Climbing into the saddle, Deputy Sheriff Martin Greer soldiered on.

He'd bring Miller back to town later. With his brother.

Or he wouldn't. Because maybe Greer would end up dead too, and then it wouldn't matter.

But he'd die before he let another poor girl be hurt by the monster in Seth Miller's cellar.

When he got to the Miller claim, a row of wooden Indians caught his attention.

In various stages of completion, the carved figures lined the long front porch of Miller's ranch home like religious idols. Some wore traditional Lakota Sioux war bonnets. Others were bareheaded with long braids dropping over squared shoulders.

All of them had the same malevolent face that Greer had strained so hard to remember.

He spurred his horse around the house and found the cellar almost hidden in a clump of grass. A cement bump rising from the ground with a hinged door of whitewashed pine.

There wasn't any sort of lock on the door.

Greer dismounted and led his horse away, sixty feet. If bullets started to fly, he didn't want to risk a good old hoss. The bastard down there had taken enough from him already.

He withdrew the Henry from its boot on his saddle and walked to the cellar.

Rifle in his right hand, he gripped the handle with his left and swung the door up and over, letting gravity bring it down to the grass on his right with a crash.

Sunlight revealed a set of wood stairs descending through walls of brick and mortar, the bottom shrouded in shadow. No sound came up, but the stink of foul waste and decay knocked Greer back a step. How anything, anybody, could live down there was the devil's best guess.

He put a boot on the top step and called

out. "Jonah Miller, you down there? Your brother told me where to find you."

At first there was no sound, only a light southern breeze ruffling the grass around the entrance.

Then a shuffling across the floor below.

Like the scurry of rats.

Greer took another step down. The Henry was slick in his grip. The stench, overpowering.

"Deputy . . . Greer, isn't it?" Jonah's voice was calm and condescending, and it raised all the hairs on the back of Greer's neck. "I'm honored by your visit."

Greer said, "Walk into the sunlight, where I can see you."

"So you can shoot me? Why would I be stupid enough —"

"Where I can see you, damn it."

"I must have your word, Deputy. Promise you won't shoot."

"Fair enough. I just want to talk."

"Promise?"

"I promise."

The standoff lasted a full minute, seconds ticking by like an eternity.

When Jonah finally moved, it was with the shuffle again, and the clank of an iron chain.

And the face appeared at the bottom of the stairs.

Chief Virginian's face. The face of all the cigar store Indians on Seth Miller's porch.

The face Greer had seen in the moonlight the night his wife died.

He took another step down into the pit.

Jonah's clothes were soiled and hung like rags from his skeletal frame. That such a figure could pick up a knife, let alone wield it with enough force to harm anybody, challenged Greer's thinking.

Could his memory be playing tricks?

But suddenly there was no doubt. Jonah sprang forward, trailing a loose chain behind.

Of course, the chain was loose.

Jonah had been free to come and go as he pleased for a long time. Around four months according to the body count. Long enough for the seasons to change from spring to summer.

Long enough for a man to get lost and find himself again.

Greer leveled the rifle and pulled the trigger.

He unrolled the portrait of Jonah Miller on Sheriff Dodd Carter's desk.

Then he returned the Henry to its place in the gun rack.

Carter watched him, then turned his attention back to the drawing. "You finally remembered," was all he said.

"I did. And now I'm going home to bed. I plan on sleeping for a week."

Then Greer reached into his pocket and pulled out a piece of coal black charcoal.

Crossing the office in three strides, he pushed the stick onto the drawing and ground the end down to a nub. The action left a round black spot between Jonah Miller's eyes.

Deputy Sheriff Martin Greer was an artist with an eye for detail.

THE TRAILS OF WHISPER CANYON

From where Kent Logan's cabin sat in Whisper Canyon, he could hear anything that went on. Kittens at play, tomcats at war, the trickle of rain into the rush of the Sutherland Branch, and the lonesome coo of the white-winged dove.

More importantly, he could hear every word any man said at any point between the tall limestone and granite walls from the eastern entrance to the western exit and vice versa, and he could repeat any story told by travelers along the chalk-white, brush-lined trail.

There are weird places like that, especially in west Texas where the wind carves craggy reeds of stone and scoops out horns that amplify the sound. Logan learned slowly, over a period of years, that his cabin sat in just such a natural spot, conducive to listening, the ultimate recipient of stacked echoes and suppressed background buzz.

It was on the morning of Logan's seventieth birthday that he leaned back in his comfortable chair on the porch of his cabin, rolled a smoke, and overheard a plan to rob the Citizens Bank of Wayland.

Now Wayland wasn't much of a town, and the bank wasn't much of a prize. Logan had once put twenty dollars of his own money into it, starting an account for one of his children and the bank president at the time had practically bowed down. Twenty dollars being the mark of a big shot.

Logan hadn't done business there in a long time, and he understood the town's fortunes had declined even further.

Even so, it was disconcerting to hear the morning quail and sparrows go quiet as the strong timbre of a man's voice arrived clear and unrestrained.

"We'll kill 'em if we have to," the voice said.

There was no telling direction. The words bounced in from anywhere and everywhere.

During his half-century at the cabin, Logan and his family had heard so many Whisper Canyon secrets, one more shouldn't be noticeable.

"I ain't afraid to gun 'em down to take what I want."

Logan didn't like that kind of talk, and his

ears perked up as the front legs of his chair came back down on the oak boards of his porch. He stood up and carried his coffee to the front step. Closed his eyes to listen as a second voice took over.

"If we're lucky, we won't have to gun anybody. Wednesday night, everybody in town's at the church for Lenten service. We sneak in, sneak out, nobody's the wiser."

Nobody except Kent Logan, thanks to the peculiarities of Whisper Canyon.

The two men, whoever they were, eventually made camp. They laughed and joked, got drunk and told wild stories. A tall column of smoke rose out of a cedar grove northeast of Logan's porch, and he knew exactly where they were.

He just wasn't sure what to do about it.

Once, when a family of rabid coons showed up in the Logan's back yard, swaying back and forth, walking sick and dizzy, Logan shot the first two, then followed the rest into Perdition Gorge and killed every last one of them.

That was just after baby Emma was born and young Sam only three.

When Emma was eight, Logan plugged a coyote who decided to get too friendly.

A man does what he has to do to protect his family.

Standing on his old front porch, Logan looked at the old lever-action Winchester leaned up against the wall near the door. How many times had protection come with the black powder blast of a gun?

Was this one of those times? Why get involved now?

Logan had never had to kill a man. These varmints weren't a threat to his kin. And his family was long gone; the kids to families of their own. His beloved wife to eternity.

Logan picked up the rifle and decided to take a walk.

The sun was low in the sky, but it sent orange evening light through a narrow crevice in the west face of the scrub-covered canyon wall — as it did on this day, every October, every year. Logan knew every step in his dance with the sky, knew every move of the sun, moon, and stars in relation to his home.

He knew sunrise and sunset, the seasons, the planets, and the stars. He knew when it would get too dark to see in the shadows of the towering rock walls. And he knew when and where the moon would appear.

Whisper Canyon's wagon road was ten feet wide and rutted from steel rims, but it was hardly the most populated way. Logan eschewed the way of men and followed the networks of deer paths and the routes of rabbits and squirrels. On a winding trail to Sutherland Branch, he remembered the day Sam had gone missing.

As a parent, nothing prepared him for the instant he realized his four-year-old son had vanished into the wilderness. He'd been playing beside a stump as Logan split wood. The next instant, the kid was gone.

Logan recalled the lurch of his stomach. The punch to his heart. "Sam!" he called. Over and over and over, "Sam!"

And ten minutes later he found the boy waddling along the trickling spring-fed branch, doing his best to follow a darting minnow.

Sam had grown up to know Whisper Canyon as well as Logan.

Emma too.

Together with Sarah, his wife, Logan taught the kids how to use a bow and arrow, gunsmithing, brush craft and woodworking, and the ways of fickle Mother Nature.

A whiff of a breeze carried woodsmoke. Logan was closer to the bank robbers than he thought. As the dark of night enveloped him, he slowed his breathing and listened.

"You sure about the Wayland job, Clem? More I think about it, more it seems like a pissant of a little bank. Not near as big as our last job over in Maryville."

"Mrs. Merkle didn't raise no dummy, Mel. I figure we'll take more than a thousand dollars. It ain't Maryville, but ain't it a prize worth going after?"

"A thousand . . . ? Well, hell yes. I'm with you for a thousand dollars."

"And you ain't afraid to use your gun?"

"I ain't afraid, Clem."

Logan pressed his lips together with grim decision. Up until now, he'd considered letting the men make camp and go. Like so many others over the years, they were passing through, and Logan was no busybody sticking his nose in other people's affairs. Travelers had a right to their privacy — to their own business whether Mother Nature ratted them out via the canyon's oddball acoustics or not.

But this Clem Merkle and his pal, Mel, were a little too eager for mayhem. A bit too bloodthirsty.

Thinking about it lured his memory off again to the racoons. Which made him think about the time Emma was sick with a bee sting.

At first, it had been nothing, and Sarah had treated the welt, no bigger than a sunflower seed, by wrapping a slice of bacon around Emma's arm. But next day the puffy skin was red and as big around as a dime, then later a gold dollar, and Em scratched at it and ugly red streaks ran up past her elbow.

Emma's week of fever was the longest trial of Logan's life. The gnawing ache in his gut that never went away. The terror grabbing hold of his lungs every time Emma whimpered. Neither he nor Sarah slept. It was all they could do to keep water down — in Emma, or themselves.

Logan leaned on his rifle and peered up into the cedar grove where the bank robbers' fire flickered against the trees. Remembering his joy watching Emma run through those trees a few weeks after her ordeal, healed, healthy, with summer in her smile.

The presence of these bad men was something of a blight on Logan's good remembrance.

He picked up his rifle and walked on toward his destination.

There was no way for Logan to adequately convey his feelings for Whisper Canyon. It wasn't enough to say it was home. Having loved here and lost, he brushed away the picture of Sarah's tombstone up on the hill behind the cabin — the place was more to him than a living space. Having built roads and houses and sheds with his son, it was more than a geographic location. He'd found suppers in the brushy woods and the crystal clarity of Sutherland Branch. He'd been bitten and stung, scraped and cut, broken and repaired. His boots had trod every square inch of ground from one end to the other, and his fingers knew every rough tree and smooth stone.

Whisper Canyon was knit into his bones, and nobody knew it better.

At the clearing between Emma's mulberry tree and the north pass, he stopped and cleared his throat.

"That's right, Sheriff," he said out loud with a thick baritone voice. "Those men you want for the Maryville job are right up the trail here."

Logan relaxed against a cottonwood tree and lobbed a few loose rocks into the thicket just to make a bit of noise. Seconds later, the flickering flame of Clem and Mel's campfire was smothered.

Logan called out again, "I know you don't like to shoot first, Sheriff, but it seems to me we can't take chances with Clem Merkle. He's a bad egg. And don't get me started on Mel, the mangy polecat he's running with."

The night held its peace, and the first rays

of a crescent moon popped over the far canyon wall.

Logan bided his time, then said, "No, you're right. We've got to clean them out now before they try for Wayland. I hear there's a posse of twenty armed men waiting for them over there."

Before another minute ticked past, two riders on horses broke cover from the cedar grove and appeared on the trail, riding hell for leather in the opposite direction of Wayland, following the road back out of the canyon the way they came.

Logan smelled sage in the cloud of dust they raised, and he waved goodbye as they passed less than thirty feet away from where he was hidden in the foliage. Clem Merkle and Mel had a long trail ahead of them.

But Logan was pretty sure they wouldn't intrude on his peace, or the poor folks of Wayland, ever again.

Because while Clem and Mel had a long owlhoot trail yet to follow, Logan was nearing the end of his road. A more challenging road. Ultimately, a more rewarding road.

The bank robbers' trail was filled with pitfalls they worked to avoid, decisions that made them weak and stupid. Logan's road had strengthened him, had educated him.

He knew everything there was to know

about living in Whisper Canyon, lessons learned by raising a family there. He knew, for instance, that his cabin sat in a natural spot, conducive to listening. He also knew that the clearing between Emma's mulberry tree and the north pass was conducive to broadcasting.

That everybody in the canyon could hear any words spoken there, real or imagined.

He had a feeling Clem and Mel would be remembering and exaggerating those words Logan had shared with them.

Probably for years to come.

C — As in Civilized

A balmy Thursday in January and the Otterville young were restless and wild. Which
might not seem out of the ordinary for a
dozen children aged seven to seventeen, but
Elisha Wade had been working to instill a
sense of discipline and cooperation into his
one-room classroom since September. He
was forcing them to become *civilized.*

"Edwin Pepper, drop that jar of paste this
instant."

"Gladys Case, ladies dare not use such
language."

"Anderson Toombs, if I have to tell you
again . . ."

It went on like that all morning.

Admittedly, Elisha hadn't been much better at their age, having grown up during
Reconstruction after the war and only
recently moved to Nebraska from his native
South Carolina. But the West, he felt, was a
new chance for civilization, and he em-

braced his position as headmaster in Otterville.

He had a new life, a new claim with a house and grounds he was proving up on, and a mission.

Elisha Wade, bringer of education, refinement, and reason to the Wild West.

A man of logic, at the age of twenty-two in that year of our Lord 1888, he couldn't deny he felt an inexplicable, primitive buzz of anticipation in the air.

That pleasant January morning, the premonition was almost palpable.

Something was coming.

Something ineffable and indescribable. Something as wild as Cora McNeil deliberating hurtling a dried apple slice at Jacob Riedell.

Distracted by his feelings, Elisha's finger wag was as half-hearted as his tone of voice. "See me after class, young lady."

The headmaster's anemic request resulted in a smattering of snickers since Cora, at seventeen, was the room's most matronly occupant, and the children had long ago put her together with Elisha in an imaginary romance.

With an open hand, he banged on the lectern for order.

The students took their places on wood

folding chairs among the freestanding writing desks. The back door was secure. The enamel bucket was full of water, and a silver dipper hung from a hook on the lip. A basket of leftover dried apple slices sat under the window for snacking.

Blackboard dust and pencil shavings forced Elisha to sneeze.

"Class is now in session," he said.

He heard himself say it, but his attention was split seven ways to Sunday by the shuffling and whispering of the students. Something was coming. They felt it too.

He picked up a piece of chalk and adjusted his wire spectacles.

"Today's vocabulary words are as follows. For the front row . . . who can spell *apple*?"

The answer came from seven-year-old Edwin. "A-p-l-e."

"Close," Elisha said, and turned to the slate blackboard easel to inscribe the word with an additional letter. "A-p-p-l-e."

"Next word: *battle.*"

Again, it was precocious Edwin who spoke, this time remembering the second consonant. The word was added to the chalkboard list.

The next word was *century.*

When no one volunteered, Elisha called upon Anderson Toombs. The big boy dressed in clean new overalls was Elisha's chief rival for Cora's affection. The son of an affluent cattleman, Anderson was everything his teacher was not. Muscular, good-looking. Elisha had no doubt Toombs and Cora, both of whom were finishing their last year of school, would be married before the end of summer.

"S-e-n . . ." Anderson began, and Cora giggled from the front row, her blond curls bouncing like spring flowers along her graceful jawline.

"Go ahead, Anderson," Elisha said, but the devil had his tongue.

"I . . . give up."

Cora tucked her chin down so her eyes might flash a petulant sky blue.

She was evil incarnate.

Elisha said, "Anyone else want to have a go?"

When none of them took up the challenge, Elisha wrote the word in chalk. *"Century,"* he said, "With a C. As in *city,* or *center."* He faced the congregation and gave them his gospel straight, "C — as in *civilization.* That for which we all must aspire as a group. Many hands working together, lifting the banner of society."

Edwin raised his hand. "Mr. Wade, what does ass-pire mean?"

"Nothing less than to *work toward,* to *strive.*" Elisha clenched his fist. "To *long* for something."

"Anderson Toombs ass-pires for Cora," said eleven-year-old Gladys, and everybody laughed except for the two students mentioned.

"That's quite enough," Elisha said.

But Gladys wasn't quite finished. "I think Cora ass-pires for you, too, teacher."

Cora rose up in her seat, flushed and indignant. Before Elisha could speak, she chucked another apple slice across the room, clouting Gladys on the ear.

"Goddammit," said Gladys, "you've done it now."

And just like that, the dam broke, taking civilization with it.

Alan "Pep" Pepper rode herd for Chet Toombs and was an old hand at nighthawking. He was used to the winter cold but welcomed this morning's pleasant temperatures. Maybe it was coming up on what the old-timers called the January thaw, a few days of moderate temperatures before winter returned.

Pep rode his gelding through the forty head of Polled Herefords and swung from the saddle at the bottom gate of Looking

Glass Lane. Beyond, the open stubble field of last fall's corn harvest beckoned. The cows would quickly clean up any spillage the reapers had missed. For a while, cattle and man alike could relax and stretch their legs.

Pep opened the gate and called the cows with a whistle.

After the herd plodded through, another man rode up on a horse.

" 'Lo, Pep," Wendell Huttman said.

"Hi, Windy."

Windy wore a burlap slicker over a heavy sweater and tough denim jeans. On one side of his saddle, he carried a loop of heavy rope. On the other, a long leather boot kept his Winchester carbine snug and safe from the elements.

"You ain't wearing a coat? What'cha think it's July out here?" Windy was always one for the smart aleck remarks.

Pep tipped his head toward the sky and its patchwork of white and gray tattered clouds. "I 'spect now you're gonna tell me it's going to rain."

"Rain, storm. Somethin's coming, you can be sure of that. My old knee started singing to me during supper yesterday and kept at it all night long."

"Not a song you want to hear."

"Not by a damn sight."

Windy was ten years older than Pep, but he had only been on the ranch for a few months. Pep had taken an instant dislike to the man's snide comments and boozy breath. And of late there were rumors of cash money gone missing from the ranch. Pep suspected Windy, but he couldn't prove a thing.

Windy drank cinnamon-spiced whiskey from a dented canteen, offered it to Pep.

"No thanks."

"G'wan, take a drink. Your mama ain't watching."

Pep pretended to take a sip. Then he returned the canteen and changed the subject. "You figure that old burrhead cow is going to calf one of these days?"

"If we're lucky, it'll be today. More likely she'll wait until it's raining like a son of a gun and then go wander off and have her calf in a creek."

Pep looked at the sky once more. "Or maybe, if what your knee say is true, maybe this forenoon would be better."

Windy clucked his tongue and his dun gelding clopped through the gate into the stubble field. "At my age, forenoon is better for just about everything, no matter what the weather."

Pep closed the gate behind them, then climbed into his gelding's saddle.

The two men rode together in silence for a few minutes, Pep enjoying the mild day, watching the mass of cowhide in his keep fan out in front of him. The herd was a healthy mix of younger calves and yearlings tossed in with older animals. Pep eyed the far end of the field where a windbreak of cottonwood trees and ragged cedars grew on the banks of the spring-fed Ulysses Creek.

"Warm day," he said. "Ought to be plenty of water for the cows."

"No worries there," Windy said. Then: "You got business in Otterville today, Pep?"

Pep lined the question up in his mind, looked it over front to back, weighed it like a sack of corn, and turned it upside down. He knew why Windy asked, but he answered with the truth anyway.

"Yes, I'm going over to Otterville. I planned to call on Miss Stepanova before picking up Edwin at school."

"I see."

"And you don't approve."

Windy held up both of his calloused, tough hands to the wind.

"I don't blame you one damned bit," he

said. "Your boy needs a mother. I under-stand."

Pep felt a hot rush of blood to his face. Polina was a frequent topic of discord between them.

"She's not what you think."

"She ain't got any roots here," Windy said. "She's an outsider."

"And she works in a saloon."

"You said it, not me." Windy stared off at the foggy horizon. "I hate to see you get hurt is all. Hate it for the boy."

"Or do you hate it for yourself?" Pep hadn't meant for the accusation to pop out, but there it was.

Windy moved his jaw around, then grum-bled, "Maybe I do."

"All due respect, friend, I don't give a goddamn what you hate —"

"That ain't fog, Pep."

"What?" The odd declaration came out of the blue. "What are you talking about?"

"I say, that ain't fog out there to the north. See that band of white rolling in over the creek."

"I ain't sure what you —"

Then he saw.

And the roar of the wind almost tore them from their saddles.

If the world were just and life were fair, Polina Stepanova would be Mrs. Henry Case, and she'd be cleaning chickens and growing garden produce surrounded by a flock of Case boys and girls on a pretty little acreage north of town just like she'd planned.

Instead, the mail order bride who traveled all the way from the old country to find an American cowboy had disembarked from the train with the letters of a dead man clutched in her hand.

Twelve hours before Polina arrived on the stage in Otterville, Henry Case met his maker with the kick of an angry mule to the forehead — the kind of farming accident that happens every day.

He left behind two adult boys and an eleven-year-old girl named Gladys.

So here was Polina in the Otterville Pub serving up a mug of half suds to a toothless old man at the corner table before picking up a towel to walk behind the bar. "Hot morning, ain't it, Polly?"

"Every morning is hot for you, Gus."

"I don't know about that."

"It's da fires of hell lickin' your boots, Gus."

"You're an angel to say it, Polly. How's about you and me get hitched?"

It was the same banter they traded every morning.

"How about *nyet.*"

"Not yet, you say?"

"I say 'No.' "

Thursday was no different than Wednesday was no different than Monday. Gus McNeil staggered in early for a few eggs and toast, gummed it all to mush, and washed it down with a quart of beer. Gus was Polly's best customer, and he was usually out like a candle before noon.

To think she might've been a farm wife with children. A productive member of American society. And now, here she was playing barmaid to a drunkard.

She polished the wood counter and looked across the wide-open barroom with its chairs mounted on the tabletops, its floor freshly swept, and the lone window looking over downtown Otterville. The sun wasn't shining, but old Gus was right.

Polina had started the stove the same way she did every day in January, but with it being so warm outside, it was stifling hot inside the saloon.

She walked to the front door and pushed it open to the street.

The squawk of the door on its hinges caught Gus's attention. He stood up and carried his beer to the bar where he waited for Polina. "Tell me more about your home in Russia. What's it like back there in the savage country?"

"It is not savage. Just different. I have told it all to you before."

"I like to hear the sound of your voice."

Something about the way he said it made her feel slightly less alone. She tamped down the feeling until it went away.

"Why don't you tell me about your home, Gus. Where do you come from?"

"I'm from right here."

"You are much older than the village of Otterville on the high plains."

"See, that's what I mean about your talk. You say things in ways nobody else does." He turned his voice into a high-pitched warbling soprano. "Otterville . . . on the high plains."

She couldn't stop the laugh that spilled from her lips. She slapped his arm. "I do not sound like such a thing."

Gus chuckled. "I guess I'm not in practice. You should learn me some Russian sometime."

"I should teach a horse to juggle beer mugs and have as much luck."

"You got me there."

"Why don't you ever talk more about yourself, Gus? You have family here?"

Gus nodded, slurping at his beer, leaving foam on his hairy upper lip. "I do. I got a niece I look after. Name's Cora. She cleans my house. Cooks for me. One of these days she'll be gone."

"Why gone?"

Gus tilted his head back toward the street. "She's got it bad for Anderson Toombs. That's Chet Toombs's boy. Figure them on getting hitched one of these days."

"I know Toombs," said Polina.

"Which one? The elder or the younger?"

"Chet Toombs bought me a drink the other night. Right there where you are sitting."

"The skunk."

"He is a married man?"

"He is a married man. He has no business buying you drinks. That's why I called him a skunk." Gus finished his beer and slid the mug across the bar to Polina. "Fill 'er up again."

"I think your niece would be fortunate to marry into a family with such wealth."

"Yeah . . . well, there's more to life than money. Believe you me."

"You say this because you have money."

"Hell, I don't have two nickels to rub together."

Polina raised her eyebrows. "I have never had money."

"One more reason you and me should get together."

Again, she couldn't help but smile. "You tease too much, Gus. One day I might say yes, and then where would you be?"

"I'd be in trouble, wouldn't I?"

"You might bite off more than you can eat."

"More than I can chew."

She filled his mug and slid it back to him. "Uh-huh."

"Besides, you can't kid a kidder," Gus said. "I've seen the moon eyes you and Al Pepper give each other whenever he gets to town."

"Maybe you should mind your own —"

A rolling gust of wind came through the open door like a steam train. Two chairs toppled from a tabletop and a spatter of dust rattled through the room and across the bar.

Grit bit into Polina's cheeks, and Gus lost his hat.

"What in thunder was that?"

Precisely.

Thunder was the crashing boom that came next.

When the first arctic wind hit the schoolhouse windows like a black powder blast, the students jumped from their seats. On the other side of the glass, Chet Toombs's oats field was encased in a solid white cloud of whirling snow.

Elisha shooed his students back into place. "Back in your seats, back in your seats. Surely you've seen snow before." He scurried around the room, herding his charges into their seats. This was his first winter in Nebraska, and it had been colder than he expected, but he was still surprised by the clouds of vapor escaping his mouth as he spoke.

He'd never experienced such a rapid drop in temperature.

In an instant, the temperature in the schoolroom had seemingly dropped by twenty degrees and remained in free fall. "Everybody put on your coats," Elisha said.

He added, "If you have one."

It had been so warm that morning, some of the students had left their coats and outer clothes at home.

"Back in your seats, I say." Elisha turned his attention to the pint-sized tin hay burner in the back of the room.

Another casualty of Mother Nature's vile trick. He had opted not to fire up that morning — now it might be too late.

"Do we have fuel for the stove? Anderson?"

The big boy shrugged, still harboring a grudge over the spelling lesson. "Don't know."

Jacob Riedell, one year younger, said, "I can bring some in from the pile."

Elisha said, "Please do so. Anderson, you help him."

Anderson's reply was a loud, petulant complaint.

Elisha cut him off. "We're going to need to work together here, folks. Remember what I said about civilization?"

Anderson plodded over to the hangers where he'd put his coat earlier that morning and pulled his slicker over each arm. He kept a coil of lariat rope on the adjoining hook, along with leather gloves and a tall hat. In his coveralls pocket, he carried a knife. Elisha always pegged him as overprepared. Nothing but a show-off.

Right now, Anderson's outfit didn't seem so ridiculous at all.

Gladys McNeil still had her face pressed to the glass pane, and next to her were the

Schmidt twins, only six years old. Gladys said, "It sure is snowing a lot out there, isn't it, teacher?"

Elisha joined the girls and caught sight of what looked to be a solid sheet of white encircling the schoolhouse. He couldn't even see the bare branches of the mulberry tree that stood just outside the schoolhouse.

One quick look outside had been enough to pour ice water into Elisha's veins, and a steel vice squeezed his pounding heart. A blizzard was upon them, terrible and deadly in its ferocity.

A frantic, wind-whipped shroud had suddenly dropped from heaven.

"Stay calm everyone." Saying it to himself as much as the children.

His heart galloped on like a wild stallion, and his mind raced through dozens of scenarios before him, all of them unpleasant.

On Elisha's path back to the lectern, Cora lunged into his way and threw her arms around him. "I'm so frightened."

Covered in snow, Anderson Toombs stumbled through the door at just that moment, an armload of damp brush falling to the cold floor. He saw the embrace, and said, "I'm going home."

Elisha pried himself loose from Cora's

grasp. Turning and speaking to the class he said, "Nobody's going home until we go together. No one is to leave the school." Then to Cora, "Run, help the boys with the heater."

"Little me?"

He pushed her away. "I don't have time for any more of your nonsense, Cora. This is a serious situation."

"But —"

Holding her gaze with the last of his nerve, he put every ounce of authority he had into his voice. "Go. Now."

Her loving gaze turned to stone. "In my moment of distress, I should never have expected such a reaction from you, Elisha. Why, I'm so . . . so utterly nonplussed, I don't know what to say next."

Never a loss for words, Gladys said, "Button your lip, fatty."

Cora would've socked her if Edwin hadn't cut between them.

"My pa works out on the Toombs ranch," he told Elisha. "He's been in a thousand snowstorms."

"Let's hope he's inside today," Elisha said.

"He ain't. But he's tough as any old blow."

A blast of thunder rattled the windows, and one of the twins clutched Elisha's leg. "I'm scared, teacher." Elisha picked up Ellen Schmidt, and she put her head on his shoulder. He walked to the back of the room.

"How's the fire coming, boys?"

Squatting next to the hearth, Anderson's impatient squirming conveyed as much as the lack of smoke. His voice was a whine. "We're getting nowhere. Everything is too wet to burn."

"Let me try," Cora said, kneeling down beside him. "Give me those lucifer matches."

Anderson rubbed his arms through his shirtsleeves. "I want to go home." He looked around at Jacob, Cora, and his peers. "My daddy's got a twelve-foot-long fireplace."

Cora snapped the matches against the side of the burner, one after another.

"We should just go home," Anderson said.

Elisha felt the little girl in his arms start to sob.

Anderson was probably right.

If they couldn't get the stove going, Elisha would have to dismiss the class. They couldn't stay here with below-freezing temperatures and no fire.

But where could they go in the storm? Elisha wasn't about to let the class disperse in a dozen different directions as they did on a normal day. Most of them had several miles to walk between the school and their homes. They'd be lost for sure.

No, they had to stay together. They had to remain civilized.

Cora tossed down the packet of broken matches. "I can't get the damn things to light."

Downtown Otterville was less than a mile away, just on the other side of the hayfield and across Ulysses crick.

Stay? Go? Stay? Go?

The decision of what to do tapped out a beat in Elisha's head like the steady ticktock of the clock on the back wall of the schoolroom.

It might be a bit of a brisk walk, but surely they could make it to town before the storm got too much worse.

He gazed at Anderson's lariat rope hanging on the wall and made the decision.

"Give 'em credit, they're trying to bunch together," Windy said through frozen, chapped lips. "It's instinct for cows to pull in the ranks. They're just too damn dumb to know what they're doing."

Pep squinted into a hail of snow, the gathering of beeves playing out as dark, brick-red shadows in a murky field of white. "Those animals are as blind as we are."

"Let's get them into the trees if we can. There's at least some shelter there. Maybe we can drop into the creek bed."

"If we don't fall in."

Pep figured they were less than a quarter mile from the trees and creek.

The town of Otterville a scant quarter mile beyond that.

Somewhere over his shoulder to the north, Edwin was tucked in safe and sound at school. He hoped that snot-nose headmaster had the good damn sense to keep the kids safe inside. With the little school's cookstove and the bushel basket of apples in the corner, they'd be safe enough.

Pep hunkered down in his saddle, leaning over the horse's withers, keeping his cheek pressed warm and tight to his steed's neck. The gelding was fussy and confused, but it had its nose pointed toward the water. Pep gave him his head to go where he wanted, trying to keep Windy in sight.

It was slow going. The snowflakes like paper confetti stuck in his lashes, lacing his eyes shut. His cheeks were numb, and the snot dripping from his nose instantly froze to his face.

At one point, the two men were separated by more than thirty feet and Windy vanished like smoke in a rushing torrent of white.

When Windy reappeared, he had his lariat in hand. Without a word he tossed the loop at Pep, and Pep caught it around his wrist. Quick and with expert precision, he wrapped the hemp around his saddle horn.

Now he and Windy were tied together. Or the horses were, at least.

He just had to stay in the saddle.

The storm was getting steadily worse.

What had once been an easily recognizable row of cottonwood and cedar trees turned into a hazy gray blur, then a smudge of the lightest gray fingerpaint on a bright white canvas.

The dark dots that had been cows became a horizontal charcoal smear that showed for a few seconds and then disappeared. The roaring in his ears was deafening.

In a split second of clarity, he saw a red calf, not more than a few months old, running in a direction opposite where he thought the other cows were congregating.

Windy saw it too, and he used the rope to pull the two horses in close together.

"I'm going after the calf."

Pep hollered back. "Like hell. Forget the calf."

"I can save him. We're real close to the water. You can smell it."

The only thing Pep could smell was frozen

snot and the blood from his bleeding chapped lips caked onto his mustache.

"We stay together," he said. "I'll go too."

Windy wagged his head. "No sense us both getting lost." He had already untied his end of the rope, tossed it over to Pep. "Don't you come out after me."

"Windy, no!"

But the shout did nothing to pull the old man back from the void as it swallowed him.

Damn the scurvy skunk.

The pub was the first building on the east end of Otterville.

The first destination for local settlers coming into town, and the last place they would leave at night.

Today it was a weather barracks.

The first frozen travelers to arrive in the pub were relatively unscathed by the elements. The Kleinschmidts were a young couple who had tried to drive the main road east of town out to their claim. They'd been turned back by foul wind and blinding snow. Polina got them settled in at a table in the far corner with coffee, sweet rolls, and a blanket.

More people came to the door.

Seeing them, the young Kleinschmidt said, "I can help. We've just bought groceries, and they're out in the wagon — ten pounds of coffee, flour, eggs, and other things under a canvas."

Polina patted his arm. "You warm up first," she said, and another gust shook the building.

She had never heard such demonic howls. The wind of Russian winter couldn't compare.

The next wanderer to straggle in was plastered with snow from head to toe, and Polina made him stand shivering by the stove while Gus moved behind the counter to help. "I got a feeling you'll take that boy up on his offer of coffee before this day is over," he said.

Out of the swirling fog at the doorway, they watched a cowboy appear, one of the men who rode for Chet Toombs. Polina thought his name was Wilken.

"It all come up out of nowhere," said Wilken, settling in beside the stove. "One second the air was calm and warm, the next, well . . . here it was like an ocean wave washing over the open range."

Gus fed the flames with fresh split oak. "Where you coming in from?"

"Pastureland west of the schoolhouse," Wilken said. "Toombs had me fixing fence — some of that new barbed wire. When the

89

storm hit, I was halfway back to town. Nearly missed the whole damn town and wandered out onto the prairie. If I hadn't run smack-dab into your privy out back, Lord knows where I'd be. Likely still wandering around like a drunken mule."

Polina said, "What about the school?"

"What about it?"

"The children? Were the children safe?"

"Can't say as I know. I seen 'em all outside playing when I first showed up this morning. Then I heard the bell call 'em inside."

He turned his face right, and then left. "You're gonna have a full house in here 'fore long." He stood to help with the wood. "Let me get that, old-timer."

"I'd be obliged," Gus said.

"I hope that schoolmaster had the good sense to let the kids go home as soon as the storm hit. Between you and me, that little heater they got couldn't warm up a handful of spit. They stay at the school too long, they'll freeze to death."

Polina saw the worry in her old friend's eyes. "Cora will be fine, Gus. It will work out."

"I was thinking about Al Pepper, too," he said.

"Yes," Polina said. She turned to the

cowboy. "Al has been riding with the Here-fords at night."

"Al's an experienced hand," Wilkens said. "I reckon he's well enough. Him and Windy Huttman rode out together this morning. They're grown men. They know what to do."

Gus let his eyes move around the room as it slowly and steadily filled with snowy refugees from the street.

Polina clutched his arm. "Cora, too, is grown."

Gus said. "Ain't none of us so grow'd up as to not be hurt by this kind of weather. It's a children's blizzard is what it is, and we're all kids. With us in here and them out there? We're all bound to lose somebody."

An orphan of the War of Northern Aggression, Elisha had grown up in the middle of loss. Lost homes, lost families, lost heritage. Out here, on the newly organized territories, he didn't expect to find loss again.

But here they were.

How long they'd been walking, he couldn't be sure.

If you could call it walking.

When he and the students first left the schoolhouse, all tied together with Ander-son's rope, Elisha was optimistic. But now his legs were hard iron stovepipes caked with patches of snow, stiff and mechanical as they chuffed through drifts two and three feet deep. In other places, a blowout around a stray patch of sage revealed barren red dirt, and in these places he'd stop and hitch up his pants, pull his stiff jacket closer, and adjust the ice-crusted hemp looped through his belt.

The long rope trailed behind, looping first through the belt of Edwin Pepper, then progressing a couple feet beyond in a square knot around Gladys Case's waist. On back to the next student, and the next. Until the rope terminated with Cora McNeil and Anderson Toombs.

Bound together, the students had moved as one through the blizzard, burning daylight in ever widening circles, valiant and searching for any recognizable waypoint, a row of trees or a house or barn. They'd lost their apples, their bearings, and fairly soon, Elisha feared they would lose their lives.

His enthusiasm waned with his energy and body heat, and all he really wanted was to stop and rest for a bit.

His eyes, nearly frozen shut, saw the same thing in the students behind him. Exhaustion.

He couldn't help but smile at the irony.

Out here, on the widest of open range, where acres and acres of space beckoned . . . civilization had shrunk in on itself.

All that existed was the wind, the snow, and the rope.

"We're not g-going to make it, are we?" said Edwin, ever the boy to embrace the facts.

"G-giving up?" stammered Elisha, teeth chattering in the cold. "That's not the Otterville way."

"Who . . . . . who s-said anything about . . . . . about giving up?"

It was for Edwin that Elisha rallied his strength one last time. For Gladys, and for the young Schmidt twins. It was for Cora and even for Anderson Toombs.

"Let's try this direction," he said, striking out at what he thought was a right angle to their previous direction.

Around them the wind howled, and for just an instant Elisha thought he saw . . . but then there was nothing.

"What is it, Mr. Wade?" said Edwin.

"Nothing," said Elisha. "Nothing."

And again, he found himself thinking about his overused mantra about civilization.

What was it all for?

All the talking. All the words scrawled on

scrap paper and ledgers and even — once
— a linen napkin.

Elisha stumbled in the snow. Civilization
was a sham.

It was each man — and woman — and
child — against the elements. And each of
them came up woefully short and always
would.

It was all foolishness. Wandering around
out here in the snow. How much better just
to pull the covers up and go back to sleep.

So sleepy.

"There," shouted Edwin in his ear. "Up
ahead. There! What's that shape?"

Elisha struggled against the weight of
wind and cold and sleep, pushing upwards
to stand at his full height and face the gale.
He rubbed his eyes and blinked against the
snowy blaze of white.

There was something there!

The schoolhouse refugees found Al Pepper
leaning his weight against a solid-oak corner
fencepost. Half buried in a drift of freezing
white hardpack. Moaning, only half-awake,
the cowboy still wore his hat, and his tattered bandanna covered half his face.

A few feet farther on, another staunch
post stood against the wind. And past that,
another. And then another. Each support

doing its share to hold taut three strands of new, ice-glazed barbed wire.

All that walking, and they had only got as far away from school as the hayfield fence.

"H-how . . . did you . . . come to be here?" Elisha said, shoving the words through frayed, frozen lips.

"S-stumbled into the fence," said Pep. "Walked smack into it. Cut my hand."

Elisha saw icicles of blood hanging from Pep's wrist, caught patches of frostbite lining his face, gracing the tip of his nose.

"There's another man . . . out here. Windy Huttman. I don't know where he is."

"Maybe he too found this fence."

"Are you okay, Dad?" Edwin banged on his father's leg.

Pep looked down, then he craned his neck to look over Elisha's shoulder. "My God, man. Are these all the schoolchildren?"

"Yes, we . . . we were making our way in to Otterville."

Pep nodded, gave his thumb a jerk. "Town's that way."

"Don't know how we'll ever find it," said Elisha.

"The fence leads somewhere," said Pep. "We'll follow it. That's what I was doing." Looking down at his son he said, "Are you okay, Edwin?"

"I'm fine now, Dad!"

"I think we're . . . all . . . going to be fine."

With that, Pep's eyes were more alert, and as Elisha gazed into them something passed between the two men.

Something like *hope.*

It was just the spur each of them needed, and they passed the enthusiasm along to Edwin and Gladys and Cora and Anderson Toombs with shouts and thumps on the back.

Elisha helped the older students support the young ones while Pep took the lead, tromping down the drifts and pushing through the storm with all the strength he had left.

Slow and sure they followed the fence. Post by post. They made their way.

And just when Elisha knew he couldn't go anymore, that the Nebraska storm had really won out, they came upon an out-house.

And the Otterville Pub.

Gladys Case was missing.

At some point after the students joined Al Pepper but before they arrived in Otterville, the little girl had come untied from the rope that kept them all traveling together.

"A hell of a blow after the ordeal we've

already suffered," Pep said as Polina bandaged his hand. "Keep pressure on it to stop the bleeding," she said. "I'll check on it later."

"We need to find Gladys," Elisha said, through chattering teeth. He bent under the strain, but he didn't break. "I need . . . to go back into the maelstrom."

"You ain't going alone, boy," an old man behind the saloon counter said. "Nobody goes outside into that misery alone."

The room was rank with the smell of steaming flannel and wool outerwear drying by the woodstove. Stinking with the ripe smell of fried eggs and overcooked coffee. Elisha steeled himself for the task at hand.

Polina came from around the bar, "I'll go with him, Gus." She was dressed in heavy wool with a long red scarf tied around her neck and chin.

Elisha acknowledged the Russian woman with a nod and climbed to his feet, his fingers still wrapped around a tin cup of boiling hot coffee. He drained the cup, oblivious to the burn. "I'm going."

Halfway to the door, Anderson Toombs stood in his way.

"I'll go with." For once, his voice lacked the pampered whine of a rascal. His words were steady. Strong.

Cora stood beside him, her slender fingers gripping his fat knuckles. "I'll go as well."

The old man from the bar said, "Cora Jean, no."

"She's a child all alone," Cora said. Then, quietly, "I know what it feels like."

"We both know," Polina said. She pulled her scarf up tight to her chin and set a knit hat tight to her head. "If there's any chance at all . . ."

"We need to go," Elisha said. He put out his hand, and Anderson gripped it tight.

"C — for civilization," the student said.

Against the wind, the four of them shouldered away from the pub toward the open prairie.

They woke up that morning in Otterville, a progressive little town above the Niobrara River, growing in population, thriving on the local farm and ranching economy — with all the conveniences of an industrial society. Good food, water, and health.

They had been reduced to ants, foraging blindly through an unknowable universe, their lives hanging on every decision they made.

Again, they were tied together with rope, but they were also bound by community.

For the first time, Elisha Wade felt like he belonged.

He shouted instructions over the wind. "Gladys was with us when we reached the end of Toombs's fence. She was with you, Cora."

Cora said, "We saw the little twins struggling through a drift and went to help them."

"Helping the twins — is that when she untied herself from the guide rope?"

"It must be. I didn't see." Cora rubbed her snow-spackled face with the back of a yarn mitten. "I thought she was behind me."

"Don't fret. We'll get her back."

Anderson took a perpendicular step to their trek, "I think the street goes back this way."

Polina agreed. "He is right."

Elisha and Cora took the lead with Anderson and Polina following.

After another eternity, they found themselves lost in an endless, blowing, shifting veil of white. Their feet sank deep into the snow and walking soon became impossible. Elisha pushed through drifts more than a foot high, and their path filled quickly behind them.

"We have to go back," Cora said. "We'll be lost out here."

"A little longer," Polina said.

Elisha traded a nod with Anderson.

"Cora's right, Polly. We can't go on."

"Just a little more."

Polina's history with Gladys and the Case family was etched into her face with frozen lines of worry. Elisha knew she had traded letters with Henry for several months before arriving in Otterville, only to find him dead. But she'd heard all about Gladys and the other Case family members. She'd come to know them. To care about them.

"Another five minutes," Elisha said, "Then we —"

"There!" Cora said, pointing to where a fuzzy shadow moved in the swirl.

"It's Gladys," Anderson said. "By God, it's our girl."

The four searchers nearly fell over one another in their haste to intercept the dogged, slow walk of the bawling, snow-covered child. Joining her, they threw their arms around Gladys and one another, laughing, crying.

"How do we find our way back to town?" Cora asked, and the cheers of the group fell silent.

"We follow this," Anderson said holding up a line of rope. "Before we left, I remembered Mr. Wade saying in class that civilized societies had sewage systems, so I tied the other end of this rope to the doorknob on the privy behind the pub."

Windy Huttman had planned to disappear anyway.

That warm winter morning had spurred him into a rash act, scooping up another handful of coins from Toombs's center desk drawer where the cowman kept his emergency cash.

It was the third time he'd snuck a hand into the till, and Windy hadn't been careful the first two times.

One of these days, he was going to get caught.

Time to call it a day. Toombs didn't like him much, and Al Pepper was a thorn in his side. With a pocket full of coins, it was time to move on from Otterville, leave civilization behind for a while.

Windy wrapped his frozen lips around the neck of his dented canteen and licked the remnants of drunken cinnamon from the steel. Empty.

Damn.

Windy tossed the canteen into the air, and it faded from view.

As it disappeared, Windy laughed to himself — now he was a thief and a magician!

Wandering alone in the middle of an ivory whirlpool of ice and wind, disappearing was the easiest thing in the world.

Like falling off a horse.

Struggling to catch his breath, sick with the cacophony of wind in his ears and whiskey sloshing through his guts, it was only by accident he caught sight of Ebenezer Johnson's split-rail fence.

Half buried in wind-polished drifts, Windy remembered the fence from his boyhood, before he'd been forced to move away by the sheriff and live in the Territorial Prison.

Even though it was gray, shrunken, and falling apart, Windy had no doubt this was the same wooden landmark he sat on with the other boys in school, trading pocket-knives and tossing apples at the girls.

In fact, he thought, the schoolhouse wasn't far away. Maybe half a mile perpendicular to the direction he walked.

But still an eternity's flight in the middle of a blizzard.

The fence on the other hand . . . the fence gave him hope.

"You want good neighbors," he mumbled to himself, "you build good fences." You keep to yourself, and you keep people away. Windy Huttman's motto.

He let his frost-numb fingers trail along

the top-most frigid, hard fence rail.

Carried by the storm, memory told him Ebenezer's claim was at the end of the rails. Following the fence, he'd come to the old, rundown claim everybody called Johnson's Home. The old man had never improved the place, letting racoons and worse squat inside the house with him. Windy imagined the wrecked domicile wouldn't be much good on a day like today.

But Ebenezer had a solid barn. And two or three dirty, ancient haystacks he never used.

Eternal as the pyramids of Egypt, those haystacks predated Otterville. They'd still be standing long after the town was gone.

He remembered when he and the other boys from school had played on them, oblivious to stickers and burrs, ignoring the dirt and the itchy welts raised on bare arms and legs. They climbed up and slid down and buried themselves in hay.

Buried.

With a surge of will, Windy cracked the cold sarcophagus of snow around him to move along the fence. How long had he been motionless? Five minutes or five hours?

It was still daylight, still only just after-noon. Plenty of time to follow the fence and get to Johnson's Home.

Once there, he'd burrow inside the hay and ride out the blizzard. He'd count the coins in his pocket and make new plans.

Snug and secure inside a cocoon of dusty dead grass from a past harvest older than he was, Windy would go it alone, as he always had. The rest of humanity be damned.

One foot in front of the other. Pushing past the limits of exhaustion. Past the edge of consciousness.

In the end, at the broken remnants of the fence row, he saw the red calf. The silly, stumbling bawler he'd used as an excuse to break away from Al Pepper. "You look . . . like I feel," he said, the words like hard gravel clicking together inside his throat.

He choked on a fresh burst of snow, and then the calf was gone.

And so was the fence. He'd reached the end, and the haystacks were missing.

Dizzy, Windy spun in a circle, trying to right himself in the whirlpool, desperate to get his bearings. He'd been away a long time in jail, and — a scrap of memory: hadn't he heard somebody bought Ebenezer Johnson's old claim?

By damn, it was true. The schoolteacher owned it now!

Elisha Wade, the schoolteacher, had finally

removed the old haystacks and started taking down Johnson's fence.

Windy remembered it now.

But all alone, there was nothing he could do.

HARD TIMES FOR THE VANILLA CREAM KID

It was a hot July day when Cuss Meller, whose real name was Leonard; Black Robert, who we called Angry Bob; and me, Ted Walker with no moniker, wandered into Freeburg, Nebraska, with nothing but a few coins in our pockets left over from a late-night bank job in Sydney. The trail dust was thick on our clothes, and we had plenty of time to kill. We snoozed the hot, sticky nights away outside of town near Bose Creek, but during the day we lounged around the saloon waiting for some action.

Freeburg, Nebraska, was just the opposite of action.

Truth be told, all three of us boys were sorta the opposite of each other. Cuss Meller enjoyed cooking up schemes. Angry Bob liked to sulk. I fooled around with the idea of getting a job and going straight.

Our third morning in town, sipping our first beers, aka: breakfast, Cuss got to gazing out the open door of the saloon. Heat waves shimmered off the hardpan street, and the townsfolk passing by were already wet with sweat.

Cuss sat there like a statue. You could imagine the birds perching on his poked-out lip, he was so entranced.

"What'cha lookin' at, Cuss?"

"Been studying on the bank across the street."

"I've been watchin' it too," Angry Bob said.

Which wasn't at all true, but Bob went along with everything Cuss said.

"You got any ideas, Ted?"

I had to admit, "Haven't paid much attention to the bank." I was thinking about hanging up my outlaw guns. But I wouldn't say it to Cuss. Instead, I turned my attention to the single-story brick bank building with its long front boardwalk and wide-open doors.

By ideas, Cuss meant how we might rob the place.

"What about you, Bob?" Cuss said. "Any ideas?" Bob sat on his stool like a turtle on a fence post. Asking Bob just about anything was next to worthless.

"You're the brains of this here outfit, Cuss," I said, sipping my beer. "You tell us."

Encouraged by the compliment, Cuss said, "I don't figure you fellas have noticed, but next door to our saloon here is a bakery."

In fact, I had noticed, and Bob had too. How could a man fresh off the trail not notice the warm smells filling the streets of Freeburg? Sourdough bread, cinnamon rolls, and sweet powdered sugar pastries. My mouth watered, but I had been trying to ignore it.

"Pastries cost money," I said. "Truth is, we're down to our last few dollars."

"Money's what I'm aiming to get," Cuss said. "And here's how. Been watching the bank real close. Every morning a boy leaves the bakery next door and crosses the street to deliver a breakfast tray full of goodies to the bank lobby."

"Yes, he does," I said. I'd seen it myself. The boy couldn't have been more than ten years old, and he struggled with the awkward load of three to four dozen rolls as he crossed the street.

Cuss continued to explain his plan. "Each morning the bank gives out complimentary pastries to its patrons. Around about noontime, the boy goes back to pick up the empty tray. But I've noticed it's never completely empty. There are generally five to six leftovers. Those extra rolls — he carries 'em over and tosses them into the alleyway between the bank and the opera house for a passel of stray cats."

Bob and I must've had the same expression of amiable confusion on our face because Cuss looked back and forth between us and gave a big sigh. It was clear we didn't understand.

Bob spoke up first. "I guess I don't see how we'll be getting too much outta this, Cuss. Not unless we were the cats, of course."

Cuss's face lit up like gunpowder at a campfire. "That's it exactly. Like we were the cats."

I had no idea what he was talking about, but that afternoon Cuss and me left Angry Bob at the crick with our horses and walked into town.

Cuss was dressed same as before, but he'd laundered his pants in the creek and wore his Sunday white cotton shirt with a fancy string tie — the one with the turquoise brooch he'd won in a poker match. He encouraged me to dress nice too, so I threw a topcoat over my butternut trousers and spit-shined my boots.

No gunbelts. No black cowpuncher hats.

"Howdy do," Cuss said to the jolly fat

cook inside the bakery. The door was standing wide open, like every other place in town.

"Hello to you," the bakery man said, with a deep accent. "What can I do for ya?"

The emporium was narrow and deep, stretching away from the sunlit windows facing Freeburg's main street into a dim recess of hot ovens and flour dust behind a counter with cash register and curved see-through display.

Under the polished glass, a half-dozen sugared doughnuts remained. A handful of apple fritters. And two long, narrow confectionaries topped with white frosting and a creamy goo seeping out from the end.

"What do you call that offering, there?" Cuss said. "The ones with the filling inside?"

The baker smiled. "Our specialty, the vanilla cream éclair."

"May I?"

"Of course." The baker was all too happy to serve up the treat on a clean, linen napkin. "May I suggest a cup of coffee?"

"Don't mind if we do," Cuss said.

I followed him to a small wooden table with a chair on either side where he put the éclair down like it was a valuable gold artifact.

We sat in the afternoon sunshine and watched the bank across the street. Customers walked to and from the open lobby, and if you squeezed your eyelids halfway shut you could just make out the front counter and open vault behind.

After our host delivered steaming tin cups of coffee to us both, Cuss lowered his voice. "This is damned neared perfect, Ted. We've as good as got the contents of that bank vault in our paws."

"Sounds okay," I said, but my heart wasn't really in it. And I had no idea what the bakery had to do with anything.

He nodded at the pastry on the table between us. "How many gold eagles you think that thing would hold?"

"On top?"

"Inside," he said, like he was revealing a religious truth. "Take out the custard, fill the inside space with coins. How many?"

"Hmmm . . . maybe . . . three or four?"

"I think six. I mean if you really stuff 'em in there."

"What're you gonna do with the vanilla cream?"

"There's the beauty," Cuss said. "You eat it." He dusted his hands. "No fuss, no muss."

"I'm still not sure on the details."

Cuss indicated a sign on the bakery counter I hadn't seen. It read "Help Wanted."

"We're going to go to work, Ted. Both of us."

"Work? You mean, legitimate jobs?"

"I know you've been pondering the straight life for a while now." He gave me the skunk eye. "Come on, you can't deny it."

"Darn you, Cuss. You know what I'm thinking sometimes before I'm thinking it."

"This here situation will kill two birds at the same time. Here in the bakery, you'll get a reminder on why a so-called honest day's work is for dummies, and we'll likely score close to a thousand dollars in loot."

"If I sign on with the bakery, what're you going to do?"

"Turns out that banking is more along the lines of my chosen field. I happen to know they're looking for help, too."

Before I could ask about Angry Bob, Cuss filled me in. "I've already got Bob in on the whole thing. He'll be watching the horses, guarding over our guns, and keeping camp for us outside of town."

"I'd rather work in the bank, if you don't mind."

Cuss wagged his head. "Nope. It won't work out that way."

"Why not?"

"You don't have a trustworthy face."

"And you do?"

"You have the face of a baker, Ted."

I wasn't sure if that was a good thing or bad thing, but I was about to find out.

"More coffee, gentlemen?" said the baker.

I cleared my throat. "May I ask about your help wanted sign . . . ?"

And so I became a baker's apprentice.

As I settled into my new line of work, the weeks flew past. The proprietor's name was Leopold, and he was Russian, and as nice a fellow as you could imagine this side of the Missouri. Turns out, he spoke less English than I had at first surmised, so after a while, once I had learned how to measure out the ingredients and stir the dough and fire up the ovens, Leo switched up positions and had me working up front.

It was at the counter of the Freeburg Bakery where I found my true calling, not as a baker, but as what you might call a "people person," sort of striking up conversations with folks as they came in off the street.

Leo liked devoting more time to his confectionaries, and I liked jawboning with the customers.

I was two peas in a pod with old man Linsenbardt and enjoyed Bill Weber's jokes. Jimmy Reynolds was a pal, and Miss Margaret Smith, the preacher's daughter who let me call her "Meg," was a real peach. My true confidant, however, was Mrs. Griggs of the New York City Griggses moved West. When her Griggs tongue wasn't wagging, her Griggs ears were perked up, and her eyeballs on constant back and forth.

Mrs. Griggs knew all there was to know about Freeburg. Between her daily visits for a sticky bun and my own reconnaissance from my perch on the counter, we kept good track of my saddle pard, Cuss Meller.

The middle of my fifth week with Leo, Mrs. Griggs came in and shared the news. "Your friend Mr. Meller has been promoted by the bank."

"Do tell?" I wasn't the least bit surprised because Cuss had been anticipating just such a move for the past week or two, and almost every night over the campfire he pounded his chest about his friendship with the bank president.

Griggs confirmed the truth behind the bragging. "Seems he's earned the full trust of Mr. Wesson. Quite an accomplishment in such a short time."

"Mr. Meller's a talented young man," I said.

"He has talent, that much is for sure." She said it like her meaning cut two ways. "But he'd best be careful, Mr. Wesson is not a man without resources. He's of the —"

"Smith and Wesson legacy," I said, finishing the sentence for her. "I know."

In fact, the bald little banker's claims to shirttail relations with the famous gun manufacturer were dubious.

But Cuss believed him and apparently so did Mrs. Griggs.

"Let's just hope Mr. Wesson never has reason to resort to firearms," she said, lowering her voice to a whisper.

"Excuse me, ma'am?" The comment coming out of the blue the way it did.

"Your Mr. Meller ought to know, our bank president is a crack shot."

The news didn't exactly cheer me.

Later on at the campfire, I told Cuss and Angry Bob exactly what Mrs. Griggs had said.

"You sure you know what you're getting into here?"

Cuss waved away Bob's concern. "You're just impatient, Bob."

"Damn straight, I'm impatient. It's been five weeks, and I've got nothing to show for my time but a new tobacco habit and old clothes that smell like horses. Ted here has gained ten pounds at the bakery, and you're starting to talk with an eastern accent from spending all that time at the bank pretending to be a muckety-muck."

"Tut tut," said Cuss, and it was just the proof Bob needed.

"See what I mean?" he said to me.

Before I could agree, Cuss stepped back in. "Okay, boys. We move on the bank tomorrow."

"Tomorrow?" The immediacy of the thing took me by surprise. "Are you sure we don't need more time?"

"Any more time, I'm gonna have permanent sores on my butt from sitting around so much," Bob said.

"Always Angry Bob," I said.

"He's right, though, Ted." Cuss filled his voice with solemn wisdom. "We can't put it off any longer."

Images of my daily routine, now familiar and beloved, flowed through my mind. Rising three hours before the sun, walking into town to stir the batter and heat the lard kettle. Firing the cookstove and frying the doughnuts. Mixing up the vanilla cream, filling the éclairs, chatting with Leo when he wandered in to open the front door.

My mouth engaged before my brain could stop it. "I'm not sure I want to leave town."

"Not leave town?"

"Freeburg has more or less become my home. The job, the people . . ."

Cuss lowered his eyebrows into an angry face. "As you well know, the job has always been to relieve the bank of its gold coins. As for the people, they'll turn on you the minute they realize what's happened. Your old Russian buddy, Leo, will be first in line to sock you in the jaw."

I recalled Leo's big fists punching down the risen bread dough and winced.

"Just the same, I'd best sit this one out. Bob can take my place."

"Oh, no," Bob said. "I don't know anything about your bakery business."

Cuss sat at the fire, quiet and reserved as the flames cast an orange glow on his face and sent showers of sparks toward the night's full moon. "One thing you shoulda learned by now, Ted. Being an outlaw's not for the squeamish."

Finally, after taking the measure of us both, he said, "All you have to do is load up four dozen vanilla cream éclairs to a silver tray and step in for your regular delivery boy. You'll carry them over to the bank."

"Uh, actually we have a wheeled cart

117

now," I said. After watching Leo's young son struggle with the awkward tray, it was one of my first suggestions for improvement.

Cuss nodded. "A cart works all the better. Especially when I'll need to bring the pastries inside the vault."

"The bakery side of things is up to Ted," Bob said. "I shouldn't have to be involved."

"One of you has to do it. I don't care which." Cuss continued describing his plan. "Once the éclairs are parked in the bank lobby, I'll take over, wheeling them around on your cart, handing a few to customers. Then I'll go behind the counter and drop off a sample with Mr. Wesson. Once past his desk, I'll find a reason to visit the vault where I'll accidently pull the door shut and lock myself in."

We'd heard the plan a million times, but Bob still nodded with renewed affirmation.

"And by the time anybody notices and rescues you, the filling of the éclairs will be replaced with gold coins." Then he asked, as he always did, "Are you sure you can eat that much vanilla cream, Cuss? In such a short time?"

"You know what Cuss is short for, don'cha, Bob?"

"Cusstus?"

118

"Custard," Cuss said. "It's my middle name. My full signature is William Custard Meller. Tell me this entire job ain't practically preordained."

"It's absolutely preordained," Bob said.

Both men turned expectant faces toward me.

"I won't go back on my word," I said. "I'll deliver the éclairs as promised."

For once, Bob looked happy. "Good for you."

Now it was my turn to be angry.

Cuss said, "Let's crack open a few stoppers of beer before we hit the bunk."

Thinking about the morning's job, my stomach was already starting to tie itself in knots. "I'd rather not."

"Suit yourself." He picked up a crock from the ground beside him and pulled the cork. Then he took a long, slow, pull. In the firelight, he was like a drunken devil in one of those old country paintings, and I could almost see his potbelly swell.

As Cuss passed the jug to Bob, I had a suggestion. "I don't have to fill the éclairs with vanilla cream. I could deliver them empty. That way you wouldn't have to scoop out all the filling and eat it before putting in the coins."

"Wouldn't work, Ted. If someone snagged

an éclair on your way in and they found it was empty, Wesson and the others would know something was up right off. No," he said, "You just fill those éclairs with the vanilla cream, and I'll do the rest." He chuckled. "Yes, sir, that's me. The Vanilla Cream Kid."

"They'll likely tell your story all across the West," Bob said.

"I'll be remembered in the history book of heists," Cuss said, lifting the beer back to his lips.

"You best hold back on that beer. Save room for tomorrow," I said. "Custard being your middle name or not."

The next morning was so hot you couldn't walk barefoot on the sod without burning your toes. By the time I had the vanilla cream éclairs ready to go, I was afraid they'd curdle before I got them across the street to the bank.

I admit, it wasn't the only thing I feared.

Leopold came up behind me as I added the last éclair to my wheeled cart's golden-baked and sugar-frosted pile. The Russian slapped my back. "It's as good a batch as we ever baked, yes?"

The air was thick with the sweet smell of vanilla and sugar, and I could almost taste the warm filling bursting out the ends of each roll.

Outside, the buzzards circled upwards on warm currents of shimmering air.

"It's a good batch," I said.

"It's good to have you with us," Leo said. Almost like he knew I'd never be back.

Because once Cuss locked himself in the vault, once he'd eaten the cream and replaced it with coins . . . why then it was up to me to quickly wheel the unlikely pile of leftovers outside and down the boardwalk, where I'd toss them to the cats.

Only there wouldn't be any cats.

What there would be is Angry Bob with a sack.

And then all three of us would have less than twenty minutes to ride out of town before the theft was discovered.

At least it's what Cuss said.

"See you after the delivery," Leo said, patting me again.

I wheeled the cart out into the sun.

Took a step. Then another. Wanting to turn back. Dawdling, I admit.

The thing is, I'd found a home in Freeburg, Nebraska, with Leo and Mrs. Griggs, Jimmy Reynolds and sweet Margaret Smith, who let me call her "Meg." I couldn't bear to imagine what they'd think of me once they realized I was part of the bank heist. They'd think I had just befriended them in order to play them as fools, which wasn't the case at all.

And that's when it hit me like a slug from one of Mr. Wesson's revolvers.

I didn't have to be complicit.

I had yet to do anything wrong.

So far, all I was doing was what Leo paid me to do. One foot after another, my job was delivering cream-filled éclairs to the bank.

Once there, Cuss would take the pastries and do with them as he would.

If he was capable of making the swap inside the vault, he was certainly capable of wheeling the cart back outside and down the boardwalk.

All I needed to do was park the cart in the bank lobby and make myself scarce. If I had to make excuses later, I could always tell Cuss that Leopold had called me back.

The realization of my own autonomy added a new spring to my step. The sun no longer beat down mercilessly on my shoulders. Instead, I raised my face, caught a light northern breeze, and practically danced a jig maneuvering the cart onto the boardwalk.

My friend Bill Weber met me at the door,

and I gifted him a fresh éclair in trade for a joke. "You hear about the fellow who dreamed of taking a vacation on the sun?"

"No, I hadn't heard. What about it?"

"He decided it was too hot, so he'd only go at night."

A real knee-slapper if you heard it in person, and it was just the exchange to nail in place my resolve. I stepped inside the shady lobby with its brass and walnut banisters, its marble counter tops and leather upholstered chairs.

And came face to face with Cuss Meller. "I'll take it from here, friend," he said, putting a hand on either side of my cart.

I smiled weakly, watching him push the cart through the swinging teller door with a whistle and into the back of the bank. Only one éclair had been given away. Two if Cuss dropped one off with the president on his way to the vault.

That left forty-six helpings of vanilla cream to spoon out and consume. Forty-six baked dough casings to fill with coins.

Cuss continued to whistle, but I couldn't see him as he moved behind a room divider in back.

Now was my chance to turn tail and run.

But I couldn't. I had to stand and watch the drama play out.

The big open vault waited patiently for Cuss behind the counter where one of the young tellers worked steadily, ciphering with a short stub of pencil. He raised his chin to notice me, and I waved.

"Hot one out today, ain't it?" he said.

I assured him it was, and the whistling grew louder.

Cuss was back, handing the teller an éclair and tossing me a wink. "Oh, what's that?" said Cuss. "Of course. I'll get that for you from the vault. One moment."

Mouth full of éclair, the teller raised a hand to question the comment. Together, the two of us watched Cuss wheel the cart into the vault. The teller shrugged and went back to eating his éclair with his left hand and his ciphering with his right hand.

I stood in the lobby, counting the seconds, watching the big door of the vault.

Thirty seconds, a minute. Two minutes.

Cuss tiptoed to the door, grasped the interior handle, and quietly pulled the door shut with an almost inaudible click. Even as he locked himself in, I saw his cheeks, puffed out and no doubt full of vanilla cream.

The teller was indifferent, but the heist was underway.

I turned to make my escape and came face

to face with Miss Margaret.

"Good morning, Ted," she said, her bashful blue eyes sparkling with a bounty of daylight.

"M-miss M-m-margaret."

"Meg," she said.

"Meg. Of course."

She bent slightly at the waist to look past me. "Making deliveries this morning?"

"I . . . am . . . that is . . . was . . . er . . ."

Meg had this effect on me anyway, tying my tongue and stomach in knots. I broke out in a shirt drenching sweat.

"Oh, my poor boy. Are you quite alright? You look overwrought."

"I'm fine. Just . . . my but it's a hot day, isn't it?"

"It is, indeed," she said. "And I can't imagine working in that cramped little bakery with those hot ovens." Again, she peered over my shoulder, "Or even inside this stuffy old bank. Why it must be more than a hundred degrees inside the vault."

"One hundred degrees," I said. "I . . . wouldn't be . . . surprised."

And even as I agreed, I thought I made out the first, strangled cough followed by a shushed *urp* from the other side of the vast steel door.

I remembered all the beer Cuss consumed

the night before. All the vanilla cream he'd just hurriedly swallowed. All the heat churning up poor Cuss's gullet.

From inside the vault, I heard Cuss retch again, this time with a loud cough he couldn't disguise.

For an instant, the teller raised his head, then dismissing the interruption, went back to his figuring.

"Let's move outside," I told Meg. "I think it prudent we both take in some air."

One thing for sure. Being an outlaw wasn't for the squeamish.

We moved onto the boardwalk under a limitless blue sky.

Behind, I imagined another sample of custard splattering the vault walls.

"What would you say if I asked you to the Independence Day dance?" I said, interlocking Meg's arm with my own.

As we stepped from the boards, I saw Bob, angry as ever, standing in the opera house alley, dumbstruck with an empty sack in his hand.

In answer to my question, Meg couldn't hide her smile, "Why, I'd say yes, Ted. A dozen times, yes."

I patted her hand and continued to guide her away from the gruesome regurgitation going on behind us.

If he played his cards right, Cuss wouldn't be accused of any crimes. Embarrassed most assuredly. But embarrassment beat a hang rope by a good, solid mile.

Knowing his ego as I did, I figured the Vanilla Cream Kid would move on as soon as he was liberated from the bank vault.

And take Angry Bob with him.

While me, Ted Walker with no moniker, would stay in Freeburg, Nebraska, baking sourdough bread, cinnamon rolls, and sweet powdered sugar pastries.

And if I was lucky, I thought as I patted Meg's hand, I'd make just a little bit more than that.

THE TESTAMENT OF EVE

Erna Sedlacek could talk to snakes. It was as easy and as complicated as that.

Some people had a way with dogs. Others could get a horse to listen with a whisper. Erna simply had to think, and the snakes did whatever she said.

And not just garden snakes or small-bore ringneck creepers. Erna had her thumb on the king snake and the rattler, the cottonmouth and the copperhead.

She realized the truth when she was four years old.

"Told you once, I told you ten thousand times, girl — don't pester me when I'm workin'."

Pa called it working, leaning on his hoe behind the two-story brick saloon, sipping at a bottle of sour beer, jawing with his brother-in-law, Lucas McCoy. The men were trying to grow tomatoes in a sandy garden plot.

Pa said not to pester when he was working. "You ain't never seen such a gal like I'm talking about," Pa told Uncle Luke.

To Erna, Pa's working looked the same as trading gossip.

At least he still wore his green apron. And he held onto the hoe as if for dear life as the men traded a laugh.

"Papa," Erna said, the smell of boiled cabbage from the window above urging her on.

She had been sent outside by her mother to tell the men supper was ready to eat. Lucas had been staying with the Sedlaceks in the apartment above the saloon while he recovered from a back injury.

Erna wondered how many months it took to heal a back. Because Uncle Luke had been around for almost a year without making any noise about leaving.

"Supper, Papa," Erna said again.

In the evening shade of the building, the alley was dry and hard, the sod cracking open with yellowing strands of desperate scrub grass trying to hold things together. When Pa took a swat at her, she stumbled backwards and fell over onto the New Mexico earth with a dusty thump.

Her nose filled with summer sage and horse apples from Blake Morgan's team parked in the street. She turned her head, saw the two nervous mares shift their feet around, their hooves dancing up and down.

The whirr of the rattle filled her ears.

Brown lizards scaled the rock foundation of the building, and the snake was curled up in a tight corner between a cracked hunk of footing and gray, weathered back steps.

The rattling sound was like a distant wind through the cottonwoods down near the creek. It covered Erna with an odd sense of peace.

Flat out on her stomach, Erna looked the snake in the eye.

The rattle picked up the pace, and Old Smokey picked up his head.

Without knowing how, she immediately knew the snake's name. He was called Old Smokey by all the other snakes. His wife called him Honeybunch. He was a decent sort of fellow, if a bit grouchy — Erna's impact with the sod waking him up.

She thought at him: *Be quiet. I'm not going to hurt you.*

And the rattle stopped. The curving, taut neck and arrow-shaped head went down, albeit with some reluctance.

The voice in her head said, "Assss you wissssh." The hissing, miffed dismissal of a tired old grandpa snake.

Maybe a great-grandpa snake.

Whack!

Poor Old Smokey was suddenly cut in two by Pa's rusty grub hoe, and wouldn't you know, Erna was getting the worst of it. Pa yelled down at her, "You little idiot, what the hell are you doing? Don't you know not to go playing with snakes?"

"Haw-haw-haw." Uncle Luke said from across his row of weakling tomatoes. "That's a big sumbitch diamondback, there."

"Damn thing nearly got the girl," Pa said. Then, turning back to Erna, "Get off your dumb butt and get inside."

Eyes filling with tears, Erna jumped to her feet.

She couldn't hear Pa hollering.

Not with the death knell of Old Smokey screaming through her ears.

When she was fourteen years old, Erna knew a rat snake who called himself Bob Harness because he looked like livery tack hanging from the rafters of the barn next door to the saloon.

When Pa was killed in his own bedroom by Blake Morgan that hot summer of '83, Bob Harness was as much a comfort to Erna as any dog or cat might be to a normal girl.

Normal. Like there was ever such a thing.

Bob lived in the upstairs dusty haze of the barn and ate rats and mice in the hayloft. He ate a pigeon once, or so he claimed.

Erna didn't believe him. Bob Harness was always making things up.

One day after Blake Morgan's trial and acquittal, Erna sat in the loft with her back against the north wall, cold winter wind blowing ice and snow through cracks in the barn siding, sculpting long finger-sized drifts on the floorboards. Down below, the cows shuffled through a swampy bed of slushy manure and their rough coughs sent up whisps of vapor and the stink of wet cow hair.

"Uncle Luke's gonna get even with Blake Morgan," Erna said. "He's not gonna let Morgan get away with killing Pa. Gonna strap on a gun and ride into town."

" 'Sssss a . . . baaad . . . idea," Bob Harness said. He moved awful slow in the winter.

"I'm fixing to go along with him."

"Not . . . good."

"What do you know about it?"

"I know enough. Firsssst of all . . . Blake Morgan didn't kill your pa."

"Says the serpent," Erna quipped.

"I take offenssse at the derogatory name."

Erna shifted around on the frozen cushion

of hay, feeling poked and scratched.

"Forked tongue and all."

"Excusssse me?"

Erna didn't feel the need to explain herself. She wasn't in the mood.

But she wasn't really mad at Bob.

She was just mad, and Bob happened to be handy. She took out her frustrations on him.

"It's what Pa always used to do," she said out loud, rubbing unconsciously at the knot on her shoulder where he clubbed her with a pistol butt when she was nine. "Sometimes he just took out his frustrations on other people." She scratched her arms through her heavy wool coat with damp yarn mittens, feeling the long, lumpy scar where Pa once put out a cigar.

"Ma said it was him taking out his frustrations."

"Your ma isssss a good woman," Bob said. "I'll bet she wouldn't call me a sssserpent."

"Preacher Cole told the story of Adam and Eve and the serpent in church last week," Erna said. "Your kind is shown to be lying and deceitful."

She could almost hear the snake sigh to himself. "Foolish sssstory."

"Says you. What about the apple? What about Adam and Eve?"

"I don't know applessss from acorns," Bob said. "And Adam was a ventriloquist."

Erna hugged herself against the cold and thought about what Bob said.

"You mean it was Adam all along who caused the trouble, and not the serpent?"

"Think about the men you've known, Erna. Think about the sssnakes."

Erna thought about Pa and Uncle Luke. Blake Morgan and Preacher Cole.

"Think and then make up your own mind," Bob said.

After a while, Erna knew the snake had a point.

"How do you know Blake Morgan didn't kill Pa? Wasn't he shot in the middle of the night with a Colt .45? Wasn't it a Colt still hot from the firing they found in the Morgan's wagon right there beside the saloon where he always parked it?"

The big barn creaked in the cold, late afternoon.

"That's called sssss-circumstantial evidence."

The temperature was dropping fast.

"It was Luke McCoy who killed your pa," Bob said. "I was in the saloon, outside the bedroom door. I ssssseen him do it."

Bob was always making things up.

But as the weeks went on, Erna began to

think Bob was right. Luke was more irritable than ever. He snapped at her and Ma constantly. And whenever either of them talked about Pa, he shut down the conversation with a rude comment along the lines of, "What did that old reprobate ever do for either one of you? Drink up all the profits from the saloon? Squander any cattle money we ever earned?"

Erna got the feeling Luke had harbored ill will against Pa for a long time. Now he no longer hid his feelings.

Erna went back to Bob for details.

This time when she came back to the house, Luke was gone.

"He's finally going after Blake Morgan," Ma said.

But they both knew it wasn't the case. The truth was, Uncle Luke was finally going.

Period.

Erna Sedlacek ran the saloon with her ma and a series of other girls as long as times on the frontier would allow. Which wasn't long, what with organized law and order moving in. One day the bank crashed, and they called it quits.

They moved to El Paso and worked together, cleaning the houses of rich people.

Erna lost track of Bob Harness, but never

forgot what he said he saw.

She was twenty years old in the summer of 1891.

The baron's name was John Withers, and he controlled half of every railroad running through the southeast. The son of a Colorado cattleman, Withers was young and in the market for venture capital. By the time Uncle Luke laid his money down, Erna was working exclusively in Withers's big white house on the hill.

The knock on the door came with a heavy hand one hot summer's day, not unlike the one when she met Old Smokey, the rattler in the alley behind the saloon.

Inside, at a polished walnut table Withers sipped coffee with cream and sugar.

The knock came again at the front entrance.

"Be a good girl, and get that, Erna?"

Erna nodded, scurried to the door, put her hand on the knob.

A voice in her head said, "Careful, ssssssister. Thisss man carries a gun."

A vertical row of glass windowpanes lined either side of the heavy front door, and outside on the left, she watched a light brown garden snake slither between cracks in the brick walkway.

Thank you, Sebastian.

But she had already seen the old, well-dressed man with the Colt .45 in his well-oiled holster, his cramped fingers clutching the brim of a felt hat held in front of his belt buckle. His suit coat had the faintest gray pinstripes, his trousers expertly cut and pressed. His boots, as always, were polished to the point of shining reflection.

She opened the door with a flush of mixed emotion. "Uncle Luke."

Caught off guard, Luke's surprise lit up the shadowy foyer. "I'll be damned as a heathen, if it ain't little Erna."

"Not so little anymore, Luke."

Without waiting to be invited, he snatched her up with both arms and swung her around into the foyer. "How the hell are you, gal?"

"I'm fine, Luke. I'm . . . I'm fine."

"Erna? Who is it?" Withers had joined them near the open door.

"Presenting Lucas McCoy, sir."

"Ah, Mr. McCoy. Yes, I've been expecting you." Withers raised his eyebrows, waving his hand back and forth between them. "You two . . . appear to be well acquainted?"

Luke spoke up first, taking the weight from Erna's shoulders. "This little firecracker . . . that is, Miss Sedlacek, is my niece, John."

Erna narrowed her eyes. *John,* was it?

She hadn't realized Withers and her old uncle were so intimate. Until two minutes ago, Erna hadn't known they even knew one another.

The two men shook hands, the younger towering over the older.

"Let's us adjourn to the dining room, Luke." Then to Erna, "Another cup for your uncle, Erna?"

"Right away, sir."

"And please brew a fresh pot of coffee."

Hemlock is more like it, she thought.

The voice in her head said, "Why so ssss-sarcastic?"

"Don't pester me while I'm working, Sebastian."

"Excuse me?" Withers turned at the whisper.

Erna quickly smiled. "Nothing, sir. Nothing at all."

"Bring that coffee, right away." Withers spun on his heel and marched into the dining room.

Before following his host, Luke told Erna, "I'll look you up later this evening, girl. We've got a lot of catching up to do."

Remembering Bob Harness, Erna felt a rush of emotion run through her torso.

It was Luke McCoy who killed your pa. I

138

sssseen him do it.

"More catching up than you can imagine," she said.

But poison in the coffee was too risky, she said to herself.

And too easy.

Avenging Pa's death needed to be worked out carefully. And Luke McCoy deserved the public humiliation of a hanging for what he did.

Depriving a young girl of her father. Taking away a faithful woman's husband.

She watched Luke walk into the dining room, polite. Even bashful.

Dressed in fine clothes, but more humble than she'd ever seen him.

She needed to learn more, and there was only one person to ask.

After work, Erna met her mother for coffee at the Peabody Café, three blocks from Withers's house. "I haven't a lot of time," she said. "We're having a guest for dinner, and there's a lot to get ready."

The widow, Agnes Sedlacek, was a tough nut, wrinkled and brown, forged by the elements and hardened by a life of servitude. Her skin carried a patina of pride. Her demeanor cast a whiff of reverse snobbery.

"I hope you're getting all you can out of that rich son of a bitch." Meaning John

139

Withers. "If not one way, then another."

Erna let the off-color suggestion slide away. "Mr. Withers is my friend. Nothing more."

"You got low friends in high places."

Erna ignored the insult and changed the subject. "Aren't you going to ask the identity of our guest?"

"Is there a reason I should know?"

Agnes poured coffee from the café's bone-china cup into her saucer. There, she mixed it with a fat dollop of cream. Then she picked up the saucer and made a rude, slurping sound.

"It's your brother. It's Uncle Luke," Erna said.

Agnes choked and dropped the saucer onto the table where it splashed coffee and milk across the linen cloth.

"Mother! Are you quite all right?"

Agnes waved away Erna's concern. "It's nothing. I'm just . . . sssssurprised isss all."

Erna sat back in her chair. She hadn't expected to hear the serpent's voice.

"Just, surprised," Agnes confirmed.

Erna put a cold hand to her breast. She had never heard her mother speak that way. So foreign.

So cold-blooded.

"I suppose he's still carrying around that

holster rig like some kind of gunfighter?"

"He is."

"And a felt hat? And those polished toe-pinching boots?"

"About Pa and Uncle Luke —"

"Yes, yes? What?"

"I wondered how they got on? Were they friends?"

"What kind of question is that? You were there. You remember."

"Of course, but I was a child. I don't know how they truly felt."

"There were no two men closer." Having regained her composure and her saucer, she sipped at a helping of straight cream. "If it weren't for Blake Morgan, we'd all be together today."

"What about Uncle Luke? Wouldn't he have gone away eventually either way?"

Erna saw her ma's eyes cloud over and gaze at the café wall.

Finally, she said, "I suppose he would've at that."

"Do you miss him?"

"I'm not coming over to Mr. Withers's house to see him, if that's what you mean."

"I was talking about Pa."

"Oh." Agnes was quiet again before a quick response. "Of course, I miss him."

But she rubbed at the bump where she

once broke her arm falling down a flight of stairs, and Erna decided her ma didn't mean it.

Her ma didn't miss Pa at all.

Sebastian had been friends with Bob Harness from way back in the old days.

"Heard he was scooped up by an owl," the snake said.

"That's horrible," Erna said. "He was a good friend of mine."

"I might be thinking of somebody else. Bob always could take care of himself."

"He was always so sure of himself."

"Hated winter, though."

"Don't we all?"

After preparing supper for her uncle and her boss, Erna cleaned up afterwards and then relaxed. As the sun dipped below the roofline of the neighboring houses, the two men were away down the street at the café, toasting their new business deal.

Erna wondered if Ma was down there with them.

Meanwhile, Erna made small talk with Sebastian on Withers's front porch. She enjoyed being alone with the little brown snake who rested below her in a garden of summer marigolds.

"How well did you know Bob Harness?"

she said.

"As well as I know myself. We were fine chums."

"Bob could stretch a story though, couldn't he? It's not like he was the most trustworthy source for news."

"Oh, he was trustworthy, all right. He said it like it was."

"He once said he saw my Uncle Luke kill my pa."

"You're sssspeaking about the fella who was here today? The man with the gun?"

"Yes."

Sebastian whistled, and it was an odd sound coming from a flat-mouthed snake. He waved his head back and forth in the twilight. "If Bob said he ssssaw it, he saw it."

"He was always making up stories."

"I would more correctly say he jumped to conclusionsssss."

"He was a good friend."

"The best. You've had high friends in low places, Erna."

It was like throwing a switch on one of the new electric lights. The words reminding her of something she'd always overlooked.

"Low places?" she said.

"Jussst a joke," Sebastian said. "Usss

snakes lay pretty low. Close to the ground. Get it?"

"I do, it's just something I hadn't thought of before." Holding on to the new idea like a flapping sheet on a windy clothesline, she struggled to make things still. "How could Bob have seen Luke shoot my pa from the hallway outside the bedroom?"

"The door wasssss open?"

"The door was closed."

"Bob was low to the ground. He looked under the door."

"And saw those shiny toe-pinching boots," Erna said.

Sebastian didn't respond.

Toe-pinching boots.

"That's an odd way to describe a pair of boots," Erna said. "Don't you think so, Sebastian?"

Still the snake held his forked tongue while Erna continued.

"Why would anybody describe a pair of boots that way —"

"Unlessss they had worn them?" Sebastian said.

Pa had been drinking again.

Like he always was drinking. Like he always was yelling and shouting and flailing around with his fists.

Uncle Luke got tired of it. Had been spending less and less time with the family.

Which suited Pa just fine, but Erna thought it made her mother sad.

The night he died, Pa downed half a bottle of something rust colored from under the saloon counter. He broke the bottle on the wall of the apartment and drug Ma off to the bedroom, intending to break her.

Erna's heart pounded like crazy as she followed them down the hall only to have the door slammed in her face.

Pa hollered. Ma cried.

Erna cried too, curled up on the floor outside the door, hands clamped over her ears.

After midnight, a lamp light came on inside the bedroom, shined out under the door into Erna's face.

Erna watched a pair of polished black boots tread slow across the floor, crunching broken glass. Heard a drawer open. Watched the boots go back.

Heard the single shot that killed her pa in his bed.

Erna sat up. Bob Harness was there too, on the floor next to her.

When the bedroom door opened, Ma eclipsed the lamp, the shadow of her naked, bent body inside a nightie.

"Take this," Ma said, handing Erna the hot Colt .45. "Hide it."

"Hide it? Where?"

"Doesn't matter. Anywhere. Morgan's wagon. Drop it in Morgan's wagon. He'll haul it away in the morning."

Erna did what she was told, then ran to her bed and tried to forget.

"Dumb old Bob Harness couldn't keep his mouth shut," she said, now swinging back and forth on Withers's swing. "He had to go blabbing it around."

Sebastian said, "What are you talking about?"

"Bob Harness had to make me go and remember. I really hope that owl got him like you said."

"It'ssss not like you to talk sssso mean."

"Well, of course he didn't mean to falsely accuse Luke. He simply couldn't see above a certain height."

"Not like you," Sebastian said.

"No, not like me."

"You ssssaw."

"Yessss," hissed Erna. "I ssssaw."

"And he deserved it. Your pa, I mean. He was mean, too."

"He dessserved it."

"One question," Sebastian said.

"Yessss?"

146

"What were Luke's boots doing in your ma's bedroom?"

As she moved back and forth on the swing, Erna let the words slither around between her ears without answering.

My, but it was a beautiful night.

Back and forth on the swing.

Erna decided she could live here for a long time.

She and Ma, and Sebastian, and the rest of the snakes.

All of them who lived inside her head.

THE RUNNING DAY

Jim Mallory was inside, behind worn steel bars, breathing the dry rasp of cow dust and dehydration.

And then he was out.

Just like that.

The creak of an iron hinge nudged him from sleep, and even as he rolled heavy legs from wooden bunk to stone floor, the prison gate swung away from his cell.

Outside, a cow lowed. A horse nickered.

Careful, wary, Jim Mallory let his weight settle into his boots, counting out a full minute before making another move.

When he stepped out of the jail cell into the abandoned law office, dawn hit him square in the face, and he was careful to avoid the bright open door to the street lest Merle Judd or one of his cronies take note.

Mallory looked around the room. Tried to figure it.

The night before, he was locked in tight.

Now he was out.

His eyes slid toward the cranky key ring on Judd's old beat-up desk.

Then back to the open door where the steady clop of a horse sounded soft and low and the smell of morning dew and summer crick water drifted in to tickle the scruffy back of Mallory's parched throat.

He didn't trust the lure of that door.

Didn't trust freedom offered up without a fight.

A challenge?

A setup.

Mallory strained his hearing, listening for the heavy tread of his warden's boots on his way back along the crusty boardwalk.

At first, only the rush of Wyoming wind came from the drug-out string of ram-shackle buildings outside. Then a cow made a loud chuffing sound, and Mallory wondered about the herd. Sweet Smoke was a miner's ghost camp. How was Judd's crew managing to keep them fed and watered?

Most likely, they weren't.

Mallory thought about his own treatment, how he'd been locked up in the old place for three days. Since Saturday with only a few crusts of bread and stagnant water.

Back in Sawdust City, Linda would be wondering where he was. She'd be waiting.

The whole damn town would be waiting.

The open door called to him, and he knew it was a trap.

He took the dare anyway, and striding on through to the boardwalk, eyes blinking against sun and dirt.

To his left, a familiar whinny. Spinning on a crooked bootheel, Mallory saw his roan horse first, the flash of Merle Judd's polished tin star second, the sweep of a duster and the swift lever of Merle's arm going for his gun — too late.

Mallory fell back across the threshold as booming lead sizzled past to smack into the splintered doorjamb, Judd's voice climbing over the echo of gunfire. "You seen that, boys. You seen our prisoner, Jim Mallory, trying to escape."

Two additional voices sounded from the area of the cow pen:

"We seen it, Merle."

"Damn straight, we did."

Judd's voice was full of smug satisfaction. "Looks like this here is your reckoning day, Jim."

Mallory answered back to the street. "You had no cause to hold me, Merle. We both know that."

"No cause, hell. Them's Cross Bar T cows you're rustling."

Mallory thought about the Lone Bar brand on the animals he'd purchased fair and square in Ridgeway. Since then, Judd and his men had altered the brands to convict him. The whole thing was a pretty barrel of pickles.

"It's just you and me talking, Merle. You set me up, be man enough to say why."

"That should be obvious enough, Jim. Man gets a thorn in his shoe he removes it."

"Is that how you think of me, Deputy? A thorn?"

"You shouldn't have ought to tried to run, Jim." Judd's laugh was oily and loose, just like the rest of him. "It's running men get shot. Ain't that right, boys?"

"That's right, Merle."

Mallory chewed his lip, tried to still the flutter between his ribs that threatened to turn into an earthquake. Three against one.

But Mallory knew the lawman. He knew his habits, and he knew the two brickheads he employed.

Mallory had one chance, and he'd only get one shot at it.

He ducked down and out through the door, rolling across the wood into the dusty street. As expected, Judd jerked his trigger, fast and violent, three times. Pulling to the right.

His next shot landed on an empty cylinder.

Mallory lurched to the left and pounded leather across the silt-filled corduroy road to leap behind a crooked old privy.

Judd always pulled to the right. He always fired in threes.

And Judd's two hired boys were worthless as tits on a boar.

Mallory crashed between two thistle beds into the forest.

Judd's snakelike hiss followed him into the brush. "Run fast as you can, Jim. It don't matter." The deputy hollered long and laughed hard. "We'll get'cha. You can make book on that, you damned thief."

Mallory ran from Sweet Smoke like a flame-lit cat.

"You hear me, thief? You can't steal cows and get away with it. You can't steal from me."

Mallory's legs churned through the foliage, the dry, prickly spice of pine and cedar filling his nose and throat. The rolling granite and loose shale terrain was treacherous. This high on the bluff above Moccasin River, gravity plotted against him.

One misstep and he'd go ass over teakettle.

One wrong move and he'd go down five-hundred feet to break his neck.

Judd's shout was a birdcall from above, faint behind the trees. "I'll see you in Sawdust you son of a —."

Loose gravel slid out from under Mallory's boots and he controlled the skid with a wide stance, fell anyway, twisted, and took the brunt of the fall on his left hip.

Pain, like a sober shot of hot black coffee, opened his eyes.

If he wasn't careful out here, he could get killed.

Rolling to a stop beside a friendly bear-sized boulder, he rubbed his bruise and took stock of his situation.

Gauging time by the position of the sun, he figured he had twelve hours to cross ten miles of wilderness.

No spring chicken, he was nearly forty years old. And three days in the Sweet Smoke jail left him thick headed and heavy. Like a wagon wheel hub full of sand.

Mallory climbed to his feet and pushed on, moving through molasses, joints popping, muscles slow to uncoil.

He steered toward a clearing where the rock scattered into low slung piles and shallow swales of grass bowed with the wind.

"Maaaloory!"

Judd's voice, farther away now, hard to pinpoint. Likely on the old Indian switchback that curved around to the east. Judd was a canny young hickory nut, tough seeming, but soft on the inside. His two friends were the same. They'd take a visible trail anytime rather than cut cross country.

Mallory, on the other hand, knew the land well. He wasn't afraid of it.

He surveyed the way ahead, determined to make Sawdust City by dark.

Where there was rocks, Mallory would climb. Where there was water, he'd wade. Where there was road, he'd run.

A reckoning day, Judd called it.

Running day was more like it.

Through a sunbaked oven.

Mallory pressed his lips together with determination.

That was okay. He'd been running his whole, damned life.

If only he'd thought to grab his hat from the hook inside Merle Judd's jail.

Mallory was a hard man when he was young. Good with rope and wire, tough with men, negligent of women. Expert with a gun.

Linda Swain pushed all that away, set him down on his ass and got him civilized. They got hitched and settled in Sawdust where he took a job. A good, easy job. Mostly filing official papers all day.

In the evenings, he lit a pipe full of cherry-apple tobacco and walked the long way home, stopping to talk with folks, taking the time to know them.

Tim Huttington and Ralph Barnes, Mrs. Carmichael and Trudy Snow.

It was on one of them leisurely walks he first met Merle Judd, and they became fast friends. But after Judd made deputy, things went downhill between 'em.

The younger man held Mallory's owlhoot past against him, but it was that self-same past that would beat him. Jim Mallory knew all the old rustler's trails.

Three hours into his trek, he took a breather near Broker's Farm at a clear spring-fed pool under a row of pines. Behind him, a twig snapped, and Mallory was up on his feet fast as a whip, a tough oak walking stick in hand.

"Don't be skeered, none," said a gray-bearded voice. "Ain't no call being afraida the likes of me."

From a part in the trees, a grizzled man dressed in fringed deerskin tottered out and across the sun- and shade-freckled wood lawn. When he raised his eyes, they were the burnished amber of a lion. "Damned if it ain't Jim Mallory," said the old-timer.

"Lem Broker."

"What the hell are you doing a ways out here?" said Lem.

"I'd ask you the same."

Lem smacked his lips and drew three sparkling grass carp from behind his back. "Been t'the river."

Mallory turned up his nose. "Couldn't catch nothin' else, Lem?"

"You help me clean 'em, we'll eat 'em right here."

"I've had boot leather better than grass carp." Mallory's stomach rumbled in spite of it.

Lem closed one eye and thrust out a defiant lip. "You got something better?"

Mallory had to admit he didn't.

After they ate, Mallory stood and helped his friend stand. "Wish I could stay a while."

"You never said what's got you in such an awful hurry."

Mallory grinned down into the rough-hewn features of the white-haired codger. Like Linda, Lem Broker had always seen the good in Jim Mallory, had always tried to nurture it along when all the dark clouds and bile threatened to otherwise overwhelm him. He couldn't bear to tell Lem the truth about the Sweet Smoke jail.

He couldn't bear to lie.

"I'm running," he said.

And before he could explain a peal of thunder rolled between the mountains and slapped the old man flat to the ground.

Stunned, Mallory tipped backwards on his heels, catching himself at the last second as a red stain blossomed at Lem's beltline. A second shot, and he dropped to the ground, scurrying to the old man's side. "Talk to me, Lem."

The eyelids fluttered, the breathing came in spasms, but when Lem found his sight and focused, the pupils were clear, each amber iris strong. "I'm nicked," he said. "I think. Maybe that's all."

Mallory's head was on a swivel, going around and back, checking over each shoulder. A narrow cleft between two trees exposed the spring to the wider expanse of wilderness beyond. Judd was out there. He hadn't gone by way of the Indian road after all.

The deputy was tracking him.

"We're in the fat of it now," said Mallory.

"Who's shootin' at us, boy?"

Mallory told him, and Lem let out a low whistle.

"I heard tell Merle Judd's the best shot with a carbine this side of Wild Bill himself."

"He's not as good as he thinks he is."

"I guess you'd know."

Mallory took the comment as a jab and jerked his chin toward the old man. But Lem's half-crooked grin made him bite his tongue. He caught the old man's laughing expression and couldn't help but match it. "Yeah. I guess I would at that."

Sliding an arm under Lem's shoulder, he changed his tone of voice. "We can't stay here. Let me help you up."

"If Judd sees us, he'll cut us in two."

"I ain't done running," said Mallory, "and neither are you. Not yet."

They slipped down along the side of Wallace Butte and across a long patch of open grassland. Lem's injury was just what he'd said it was, a nick, but he didn't move too fast and Mallory wasn't too eager to test the open field. The old man urged him on.

"We got no other way around," said Lem. "You go on ahead, and I'll hoof it behind."

"We'll go together," said Mallory, and the thunder didn't follow. Maybe the trip around the butte had given Judd the slip.

When they crossed Moccasin Creek at a watering hole full of ducking frogs and clouds of gnats, Mallory shared a shoulder with the old man.

At Marner Siding, Lem shared his canteen.

When they made the old line shack south of Sawdust, they stopped to rest. The sun was low in the late afternoon sky, and Mallory wasn't shy about gazing back the way they'd come.

Lem wagged his head and pulled a bite of tobacco from a mealy twist. "He ain't there, son."

"What makes you so sure?"

"We got this far without him catching up. I think he cut back to the road and plans to meet us in town." Lem shrugged. "Judd always struck me as the kind of man craved an audience."

Mallory scratched the back of his neck and sat down next to his friend in the shade of the cabin, letting the rough-hewn timber scratch his back through his sweat-soaked linsey shirt. For just a few seconds, he relaxed.

"You gonna tell me what happened?" said Lem.

"Rather not."

Lem nodded.

They were quiet a while before the old man said, "You ain't on the prod again?"

"I left Sawdust on Friday," said Mallory, "and rode straight to Ridgeway and the Lone Bar ranch to look about some cows. Ten of 'em."

"You and them damn cows."

Mallory raised his eyebrows. "What? A man can't dream?"

"These cows," said Lem. "You lookin' to acquire 'em . . . legal?"

Mallory kicked a scuff of dirt in Lem's direction and cursed. "I paid for 'em. Drove 'em halfway back home by myself. It ain't the way you're thinking at all."

"Old ways are the hardest —"

"For some people to forget, apparently." Mallory leaned forward and poked a finger toward Lem's nose. "I been nothin' but upright since me and Linda's wedding."

"Okay, son. I believe you." Lem launched a stream of brown saliva, settled back in with his chew. "You tell it your way."

"I'm embarrassed is all," said Mallory. "Shamed that a half-ass burrhead like Judd could catch me off guard."

"Snuck up on you, did he?"

"Ambushed me outside Sweet Smoke." Mallory rubbed the three-day-old knot on the back of his head. "When I woke up, it was Saturday. I was locked inside the old jailhouse at Sweet Smoke, the cows penned up outside"

"Got your horse and guns too, I imagine."

"He's got my horse in Sweet Smoke. Probably gave my guns to his no-good cronies."

Lem nodded. "So it weren't nothin' you done."

"Hell, no — it weren't nothin' I done. Don't act so surprised."

"I told you I believe you."

Mallory's voice was quiet, reserved. "You know as well as I do what this is about."

Lem chewed a while, then spit. "I guess I do. Today bein' what it is."

"The running day," said Mallory.

Lem nodded. " 'Call it that." He shrugged. "That Judd ain't been nothing but trouble since that star got pinned on his chest."

"Sorriest day of my life," said Mallory. After some thought, he took it back. "Second sorriest."

Now it was Lem's turn to raise his eyebrows. "What's the sorriest?"

Mallory climbed to his feet and put a hand on his sore hip. "The day I let you talk me into bein' sheriff."

Flanked on either side by his gunnies, Merle

Judd waited in the evening sun at the edge of town where the big wood sign was painted white and read Sawdust City in blue.

From the last high rocks above the carriage road, Mallory watched them.

"They mean to cut you down in cold blood," said Lem, lying flat beside him on top of the warm rocks. "He'll say you didn't have a bill of sale for Cross Bar T cows, which you don't."

"They changed the brands while I was locked up."

"He'll say the Cross Bar T registered a complaint."

"We'll get word to the Lone Bar foreman in Ridgeway," said Mallory. "He'll back up my claim."

"Judd's not fixin' to let you live that long. It's today he's worried about. Today he wants to win. He's betting on it."

Mallory breathed in deep.

The old man was right.

It was all about today.

Winning the day. The running day.

"What time you got?" said Mallory.

Lem took his watch from a pocket. "Twenty of eight," he said.

"Polls closed ten minutes ago," said Mallory.

Judd paced back and forth across the road. He wasn't a patient man, Mallory knew.

Since the day he'd pinned the star on the man, Mallory had watched the deputy, worked to know him. In large part, he'd succeeded. He predicted Judd would turn back and take the soft road to town, and he had.

"Alone on the road, against three of 'em . . . you haven't got a chance," said Lem.

"What's that you said before, about Judd needing an audience?"

"Am I wrong?"

"You're right that all alone I don't stand a chance."

Mallory looked around at the scrub of brush and dry timber.

"What about in front of the entire town?"

That was something else again. If Mallory could raise enough of a crowd . . .

He slid back down behind the bluff into a patch of dry sage. "Help me gather some wood and a whole lot of kindling."

"Kindling? For a fire? You aiming to set up camp?"

"I'm aiming to gather an audience."

The two men got to work, the long day catching up with them both. They stumbled through the job, building a high pile to

163

burn, wanting nothing more than to rest.

But there wasn't time.

The election would be decided tonight.

One way or other, the running day would be over.

Mallory struck a match against the wind and shoved it against a twisted chaff of brush. It sputtered and took, and he shoved it between two dry limbs at waist height. The spark grew and an eager stream of orange flame coursed through the mound, sharing heat, light, and a whirl of smoke.

"Not enough," said Mallory, fighting through a blur of exhaustion to break up another batch of kindling. "We need more. If they're gonna see it in town, we've got to pour it on."

How long they fed the fire, Mallory didn't know. Ten minutes or ten years.

After a while all he knew was the heat and the wind and the choking, awful smoke.

The first horse to appear on the scene carried Merle Judd.

"What the hell is this?" he said, palm at his gunbelt.

But there was no time for conversation.

Or gunplay.

More horses pulled in, and a wagon full of men led by Tim Huttington and Ralph Barnes.

As Mallory stumbled to greet them, Don Snow caught him in mid fall, and Mrs. Carmichael tended to Lem.

"You okay, Jim?" said Don, his gold tooth glinting in the firelight. "What's going on? Where the heck have you been?"

"Long story, friend. Long . . . story."

He glanced over his shoulder to where Merle Judd waited. Impatient. Restless.

And then there was Linda, her dress clean and straight, her strong arms around him, her smell of lavender soap and powder. He wanted only to melt into her, to let her carry him to the wagon the way he'd carried Lem across that first open field. He wanted only for the day to be over.

But there was one more thing. The reason for it.

"The election," said Mallory. "The ballots . . ."

"We've counted the ballots," said Linda, her smile big and radiant. "You won, Jim." Then her voice got loud for the entire crowd to hear. "You beat Merle Judd by more than a hundred votes."

"Which ain't bad in a town of a two-hundred-odd folks," said Don.

Everybody cheered.

"Congratulations, Sheriff," said Linda, kissing him on the cheek.

"You ain't explained about the fire," said Don. "About where you've been these past three days?"

"Time enough for that later . . . Deputy," said Mallory.

"Me? Deputy?" said Don.

Mallory nodded, the long-awaited victory pouring strength into his limbs. "I'd appreciate it if you'd pull together a posse of men. We've got a job to do over at Sweet Smoke."

He stood up straight, grimacing at the pain in his hip, and peered through the smoke to where Merle Judd had been watching from the saddle of his black steed.

There was no sign of him now. Him and his boys had vanished.

That was okay. Sheriff Mallory knew Judd. Knew what kind of man he was in a crisis. He knew Merle Judd would be running.

Trespass in Paradise

"Excuse me, did you drop this?"

The man in the pinstriped suit and gray bowler hat picked up a slip of paper from the boardwalk in front of Stone Creek Station and held it up for Bart Gardner to see.

Impatient to board the waiting stagecoach, Bart glanced over his shoulder at the stranger. "Sorry, no. I don't think so."

Ahead of him, a coach driver wearing suspenders and tall boots helped an elderly woman mount the steps into the carriage, and a bearded fellow a few years younger than Bart waited next in line beside the team of four roan geldings.

But the gray man spoke again, addressing Bart by name.

"Mr. Gardner? I'm sure this missive belongs to you."

Bart turned again. "I'm sure you're mistaken."

He didn't recognize the stranger as anyone

he'd seen waiting for the coach. The man carried no luggage.

Bart said, "How do you know my name?"

The man's dark eyes were insistent, and the slip of paper waited on the edge of his fingers.

Bart took the note, and the man spun on his heel to push through a gaggle of passengers, well-wishers, and station hands like he was leaving a firing squad.

He disappeared inside the brick-walled station without a backwards glance.

Bart shrugged inwardly. A curious end to an otherwise uneventful business trip.

He looked forward to getting home.

Bart flipped open the note and read the brief message there, scrawled in a hasty pen.

> We have your wife and child.
> Bring $10,000 to West Camp
> by one o'clock this afternoon.
> Or they're dead.

Without a second thought, Bart shoved through the crowd behind the man, leaving his travel case on the boards. Lunging through the station doors, he called at the top of his voice, "Hold on there! Hold on, I say."

A busty blond woman stumbled in Bart's

wake and dropped her parasol to the patio. "I beg your pardon, sir."

The bearded gentleman beside her seemed even more nonplussed. "You damned rascal."

Ignoring the commotion he caused, Bart pounded into the nearly abandoned station, frantically scanning the littered breakfast tables, empty chairs, and benches for any sign of his quarry.

Where was he? Who was he? Had he actually managed to abduct Bart's family?

Bart caught his breath when he saw the gray bowler rolling on its crown on the floor in the corner of the station.

He snatched up the hat.

But the gray man had vanished.

Spying the old stationmaster behind a half-wall near the cookstove, Bart called out, "Did you see somebody come through here, just now? A man dressed in a suit wearing this bowler hat?"

"Can't say's as I saw anybody."

Bart demanded an answer. "Only a few seconds ago. He must have come through here."

The stationmaster was sincere. "Nope. I didn't see a thing."

Bart examined the hat, flipped it over.

Nothing special about it. Size 7, with a

cotton tag from Line Port Haberdashery.

Bart's head swiveled to the left and right. An open side door led out to the vast Wyoming prairie, the morning breeze smelling of fresh cut hay.

Bart charged outside.

Greeted with a round of robins flitting over an immense green landscape, the view was otherwise devoid of life.

In one hand, Bart held the hat. In the other, the note crumpled in his tight fist, his fingers aching from the strain he'd placed on them. He opened his hand, looked at the note again, and then he read it a third time.

West Camp by one . . .

He dropped the gray man's hat to the ground, then walked back inside the station to look at the clock.

He had exactly six hours to reach West Camp, twenty miles down the line. Six hours to save the love of his life, and his only child, just eight years old. Who was vile enough to commit such extortion? And why?

Bart Gardner knew he was no one special. Certainly no one to warrant being singled out for such an attack.

A mere six hours left meant there was no time to think, only time for action.

The stage was his quickest, most reliable

means of transportation to West Camp, and it was scheduled to pull out any second.

But where would Bart find $10,000? The Gardner family was young, comfortable to be sure, with Bart's job, but hardly affluent. Not as long as he worked for the farm implement dealer in Green Valley.

By God, he thought to himself, if these ruffians hurt Louise or Tabitha . . .

He pushed the thought from his mind even as he shoved his way back through the gathering of well-wishers to where his abandoned travel bag waited to be loaded onto the stage.

The driver was all smiles and wrinkled cheeks and unshaven whiskers. "Thought I was gonna have to come find you."

Bart reached into his jacket and pulled out his pocketbook. He opened it and removed all the cash he had on hand. "Ten dollars to drive straight through from here to West Camp."

"Can't do that."

"Why in hell not?"

"Two stops between here and West Camp. Got passengers to drop in Line Port and a fresh team to catch at Pacific."

"To hell with the passengers and horses."

"Oh, I don't think so, sir. May I ask what's behind your request?"

Bart's mind was whirling like a steam engine with a frothy boiler. "What time will we arrive?"

"Arrive where, sir?"

"West Camp," Bart said impatiently. "What time will we arrive in West Camp?"

"Three o'clock," sir.

"That's too late."

"If you want your fee returned, I can point you to the local livery. You might rent a horse . . ."

"No, no." A horse was too unsure on the rough high country, and Bart wasn't at all familiar with the trails between here and West Camp.

The driver tried to be patient. "Sir, then step aboard, please."

Bart said, "Who's on shotgun?"

"Excuse me?"

"Shotgun. Who's your second on the driver's bench?"

"Ain't got a second," the driver said. "Just me today. Name's Brother Daniel."

"Okay, Brother. I'm going to ask you one more time —"

"And I'm going to ask you — real polite — one more time. Get on board."

Bart caught a glimpse of his fellow passengers in the corner of his eye. Waiting inside the cabin, five cramped travelers were eager to be on the move, all of them visibly restless, all giving him the skunk-eye.

All except the buxom blonde with the parasol. Her expression was one of tender concern.

"Okay," Bart said, catching his breath. Gads, but he was wasting valuable time.

What had he been thinking, arguing with the old man?

That was just it, he hadn't been thinking at all. He needed to get his wits about him, or Louise and Tabitha would be lost to him for sure.

"You win, for now," Bart said.

The driver's beetle brows came down hard over the bridge of his long nose. "For now? What's that mean? You best not cause any trouble, mister."

"No," Bart said. "No trouble."

The crumpled note inside his closed fist was like a burning coal.

The driver indicated a last empty seat at the front of the cabin next to the blonde, facing backwards. "Pile in, and we'll be off to Line Port."

Bart handed his bag to the driver and climbed into the cabin. He pushed himself down to the hard seat between the far wall and the blonde, his back to the front of the

Concord. Seated on the blonde's left was the bearded man who had referred to Bart as a rascal.

His knees rubbed with a boy blowing his nose in a handkerchief who sat across from him. Next to the boy was the old lady he'd seen climbing on board. On the other side of the matron was another youngster — a kid of seven or eight. "What's your name, mister?" he said as he picked his nose.

The driver slammed shut the carriage door, and Bart heard him climb to the driver's seat.

He felt the coach rock back and forth as the team of four roan geldings fidgeted in anticipation of their trip from Stone Creek Station to Line Port. Bart took his pocket watch from his coat pocket and noted the time. It had been nearly fifteen minutes since he'd received the note.

"What's the damned holdup?" he said.

The bearded man spoke up. "I can assure you, sir, we're in good hands. Brother Daniel —"

"Line Port's a ways away, is it?" Bart said, tapping his fingers on his knee. "Who's for Line Port then?"

"That would be us," the blonde said, indicating herself and the man next to her. She held a compact pocket mirror in her hand and brushed at her chin with a short, fat makeup brush. "I'm Betty Cooper."

The bearded man continued. "And I'm Wilcox Dierking." Bart nodded at them, then adjusted his posture and gently shifted the blonde's yellow parasol between them.

"I'm sorry," Betty said, adjusting the contraption.

Dierking said, "If you don't mind me saying so, you seem rather jumbled."

Bart saw his own reflection in the mirror, a whirl of nervous energy. His curly hair, combed down that morning, sprouted like a May garden, and though Bart had shaved the night before, his cheeks and chin were dark with stubble.

Dierking was right.

Bart's starched white collar was lined with sweat, and his string tie hung loose. He couldn't remember pulling at it. Could barely remember climbing on board the stationary coach.

But who the hell was Dierking? The man was wide shouldered, with a deep baritone voice. The gold rings on his fingers, two of them embedded with diamonds, spoke of wealth.

Why wouldn't a man like him have custom transport? Why ride a public stagecoach?

Bart's suspicions left him all the more on edge.

"Why aren't we moving?"

Even as he spoke, the coach lurched forward. Brother Daniel gave out a healthy hurrah, and the horses clip-clopped away from the rock station toward the horizon and Line Port, ten miles distant.

Wilcox Dierking said, "I don't believe we caught your name, sir."

Bart closed his eyes and deliberately slowed his breathing. "Bart Gardner," he said. "Farm equipment's my line. I work for Miller Implements in Green Valley."

But maybe Dierking already knew that?

"Ah, you're on board for the entire route then."

"Yes."

"We're off at Line Port."

"That's what I understand."

Dierking's voice was sheepish then, slightly flustered. As if caught in an indiscretion. "Oh, Miss Cooper and I aren't traveling together."

Betty said, "We only just met in the station."

Bart nodded, his eyes still shut. "That's fine."

He felt the road sliding along under the coach and continued to breathe slow.

In. Out. His wedding band tight on his left ring finger. The gold was worth maybe a hundred dollars. Perhaps a little more. A flyspeck next to $10,000.

What was he going to do?

If only he knew who the gray man was. Why he and his cohorts — whoever they were — had chosen Bart and his family for their sudden mischief. Maybe he could figure a way out of this predicament.

Maybe he could save his family's life.

There was nothing special about the Gardners. Bart and Louise met in a one-room Iowa schoolhouse, grew up together, married. They moved west and Bart looked for work, first in Denver, then north to Cheyenne. His third job put him second-in-command at Green Valley, though Miller's business was a small concern selling to a local community of sodbusters.

The Gardners lived in a nice house on the west side of town, attended the Methodist church. Before too long Tabitha arrived.

It was all Bart and Louise ever dreamed of. For them, it was paradise.

Who dared to trespass?

Maybe Dierking was one of them. Maybe not?

When he opened his eyes, Bart caught the youngest passenger again mining for gold with a finger jammed up his nose. Before he could ask, the old lady introduced the three additional passengers. "I'm Lula Matheson. These are my grandsons, Timmy and Sam."

Distracted by Betty's parasol poking at his kidney, Bart forgot the names immediately.

He shifted in his seat and pulled the parasol up from its resting spot, careful not to open it.

"I'm so sorry," Betty said, reaching for it.

Bart held the parasol up to her with a forced smile.

There was a cotton tag dangling from the handle.

Line Port Haberdashery.

Same as the gray man's hat.

Bart's suspicions shifted from Dierking to the girl. Or maybe they were in it together?

"How long have you lived in Line Port, then?" he said.

"Oh, I don't live in Line Port," she said. "I've never been there before in my life. I'm only going now to visit my aunt."

Dierking seized on the opportunity to again clear his name. "As I said, Miss Cooper and I have only just met."

Bart said, "Then it's you who lives in Line Port?"

"Yes," Dierking said. "I'm president of the bank there."

"I see. So you —"

President of the bank.

And Bart needed $10,000.

Betty took the parasol, noticed Bart looking at the tag. "Oh, I see why you thought I lived in Line Port." She smiled. "I purchased this back at the station just this morning."

"Purchased it?"

"Why, yes. From a man in a gray suit."

Bart's heart slammed against his chest. "Was this man wearing a bowler hat?"

"I believe he was."

"Did he tell you his name?"

If Betty noticed Bart's enthusiasm, she didn't let on. "No . . . no, I don't think he did."

"Please, try to recall."

"Well, I am. But I'm sure he didn't offer his name."

"Did he say anything at all? Why he was at the station? Why he was selling parasols? It's important," Bart said. "Anything at all you can remember."

"It's a beautiful parasol," the old lady said.

Bart turned to Mrs. Matheson. "Did you see this man in a gray suit, selling things to Miss Cooper?"

"I'm afraid I didn't," said Matheson. She gestured at her grandsons. "These two are hard enough to keep track of."

"What about it, boys? Did either of you see the man I'm talking about?"

Blank stares.

The oldest one made a slight shake of his head.

Damn it!

"It's this man who has you so flustered, isn't it?" Dierking said.

Without answering, Bart leaned back in his seat and let the coach sway around him. Brother Daniel was picking up the pace now.

Maybe he'd find a shortcut. Maybe they'd be in Line Port before too long.

Then there'd be a long drive to Pacific where the stagecoach would change out the team for a fresh set of horses.

Then further yet to West Camp. By three o'clock.

And the men who waited for him there. Waited for Bart to deliver $10,000.

At one o'clock.

He looked at his watch for the fifth time.

He was going to be late.

The note said they had Louise. Tabitha too.

Were they being held in West Camp?

Bart wondered when and how they had been taken from Green Valley. He saw Louise in his mind's eye, sleeping peaceful in their bed, her reddish-brown hair catching the moonlight, her peppermint-scented breath going in and out.

Then he imagined the man in the gray suit breaking in, violating the sanctity of the marriage bedroom, putting his hands on Louise, hauling her upright, dragging her across the room.

He couldn't bear to think about it.

Dierking spoke up. "If there's anything I can do to help you, son . . ."

Bart folded his hands in his lap. Looked out the side window to the right and watched the open range roll by, it's scrub grass and red clay sod flowing past as the minutes ticked away.

His pocket watch, a heavy stone against his ribs.

If only he could trust Dierking.

He might explain his predicament, ask for an emergency line of credit. A loan of cash. He could secure the $10,000 in Line Port, then maybe hire a private wagon to take a shortcut across the pass . . .

If only he could be sure.

That the other man on the coach was a banker — if that's who he was — was indeed a stroke of good fortune. If Bart had learned anything moving west, it was to take advantage of luck when it landed. He had always —

But then the thought.

Was it luck?

Was it only good fortune that Dierking just so happened to be on the same stage as Bart?

Or did the man in the gray suit already know it ahead of time? Was Bart asking Dierking for money part of the man's plan?

Bart had too many questions and not enough answers.

If he was going to save his family, he had to stop mincing around and start taking action.

Like the Methodist preacher at his church always said — he'd have to take a leap of faith.

But he could still tread carefully. "I surely appreciate your offer, Mr. Dierking. As a banker, you surely understand financial woes."

Dierking's kind features now showed a father's understanding. He was in familiar territory.

"I thought it might be something like that. The recent market strains have hit us all harder than expected." Dierking spoke over the top of Betty's head. "Does the man in the gray suit owe you money? Or is it the other way around?"

That was cutting awful close to the bone.

Bart backed off a bit. "Oh, no . . . nothing like that. It's a different matter entirely."

"I see."

"Maybe when we reach Line Port . . . if I could speak with you, privately."

"Of course, son. Of course."

The second time Dierking had called Bart *son*. The man was either a good actor, or . . . well, a good banker who sensed an opportunity to profit on someone else's woe.

"I'd be grateful," Bart said.

"I'll be disembarking at Line Port as well," Betty said. "If you'd like, we could share a cup of French coffee at the café there?"

"I'm afraid I won't have time."

"How do you know about our café's French coffee?" Dierking said. "You said you've never been to Line Port."

Bart was interested in the girl's answer. But she explained the query easily enough.

"My aunt wrote me about it. She told me she enjoys a cup of French coffee several times each week and planned to take me to the café during my visit."

"Of course," Dierking said.

Bart leaned back in his seat, planning to confide in Dierking at Line Port. Once he had the cash, he'd ride to West Camp with it.

Until then, all he could do was wait.

The landscape flew past in the windows, and the coach rumbled forward.

Time passed, and all Bart could do was think. He replayed the morning's events over and over again in his memory.

After plunging down a steep hill, the big wheels hit a series of washboards in the road that had everybody's teeth chattering. Fine dust kicked up by the horse's rough tread filled the cabin and the young boys coughed.

As the road smoothed out, the air cleared, but the older boy kept hacking away.

"Sam has battled the croup for so long," Mrs. Matheson said. "Ever since he was a baby, poor thing."

Croup, indeed. It hurt just to hear the boy's wracking spasms. And watching his face flush red at the uncontrollable strain was excruciating.

As the boy doubled over, Bart reached across the coach to put a comforting hand on his shoulder. "Hold on now. You'll be fine in a moment."

Mrs. Matheson said, "Does anyone have a sip of water?"

Dierking removed a flask from his hip. "I have a sip of rum."

"Oh, no. No liquor, thank you."

Betty's voiced her empathy. "The poor dear."

"Sam's been this way since he was a baby."

The spasms continued as the coach trundled on, lessening only a bit as they rounded one of the last curves before Line Port.

"It's hard to be so helpless in the face of adversity," Betty said. "I know how Sam feels."

For the first time since leaving the station, the youngest passenger spoke up. Popping his finger out of his nose, the little demon laughed. "You ain't helpless so long as you got that gun."

Gun?

Bart offered Betty a quizzical look.

"What gun would that be, dear?" Her voice was sugar and strawberries and cream. The look on her face was homicidal.

"Yes," Dierking agreed. "What gun, boy?"

"The one the lady has strapped to her leg under her dress."

Mrs. Matheson looked like she swallowed a bug. Her face turned pink as she stammered out her correction, "Timmy, you must not concern yourself with Miss Cooper's legs."

"But I seen it when Brother Daniel helped her climb aboard."

Freshly aroused, Bart's suspicion got the better of his tongue. "Do you, in fact, have a gun strapped to your leg, Betty?"

She was trapped between the accusing triangle of Bart, young Timmy, and Dierking. All she could do was acquiesce. "If you all must know, I do. Yes. It's a single shot pistol I carry for self-protection."

"Now you know." Mrs. Matheson directed her wrath at her grandson, but it felt to Bart like she was scolding the entire coach. "I think we'll consider the matter closed, Timmy."

Sam's coughing soon subsided, and they continued the ride into Line Port.

Betty's parasol had slipped and was again inserting itself between her and Bart. He couldn't help but wonder about the gun.

Self-protection, Betty had said. Mrs. Matheson considered the matter closed.

But was it closed?

The Green Valley stage line had never been robbed. And as far as Bart knew, Line Port was a safe, secure place to live.

In fact, the overall peace of the region was partly why the gray man's demands had shocked Bart to the core. That such a heinous act as kidnapping could occur . . .

Or had it?

Had it occurred at all?

Dierking said, "Confidentially, I don't blame you for carrying a gun, dear. One can never be too careful."

Betty's voice was full of innocence. "You don't carry a weapon, sir?"

"I've never felt the need. What about you, Gardner? When you travel like this?"

"I've never been too concerned," Bart said.

Betty said, "Your wife must worry though."

"Perhaps. Maybe a little."

"I can just see her, the poor dear. Sitting at home, praying the rosary for your safe return."

The coach slowed to a crawl and outside, Bart saw the frame buildings and corner brick structures of town. They passed by the schoolhouse and a livestock auction. The mercantile and blacksmith's shop.

Brother Daniel called out from his bench. "Welcome to Line Port."

With a cloud of dust, the roans pulled up in front of the post office. Bart hoped Sam didn't start coughing again.

"Home again, home again," Dierking said. He leaned over to speak past Betty. "Gardner, if you'd like to talk, we can adjourn to my office."

Betty turned, and the expectant look on her face was as eager as a cat eyeing the goldfish.

It took all the courage Bart could muster

to respond. "No, thanks. I've changed my mind. I've decided to travel on with the stage after all."

"You can't do that," Betty said, just a fraction too quick.

"Oh?"

"It's simply . . . I mean." She groped for the words. "I had hoped you might find time for coffee after all."

Betty's argument added fuel to Bart's convictions. She wanted him in Line Port.

And now he had a pretty good idea why.

He reached for Betty's hand and shook it. "Better luck next time."

Brother Daniel appeared and opened the door. "All out for Line Port. Next stop is Pacific. We'll embark in ten minutes." Daniel pushed his dusty hat back on his head. "Time enough to get a drink, use the privy, and stretch your legs."

Mrs. Matheson sat back in her seat. "You boys may step out if you wish, but do not leave the area."

As soon as they had permission, they were gone in a flash. "But be back in ten minutes," she called.

Now Dierking tried to coerce Bart outside. "Just a few words in private, son. I mean, if it's a financial matter, like you said, I'm your man."

Bart said, "I don't suppose it would hurt to stretch my legs."

"Of course not."

"I'll come with you," Betty said.

"But I've changed my mind about that financial matter."

They filed out of the coach, Dierking first, then Betty, with Brother Daniel's helping hand. Bart stepped onto Main Street and took in the business district of Line Creek. "The community is certainly bustling," he said. A steady banging came from the blacksmith's forge along with the smell of white-hot iron.

Dierking put his arm around Bart's shoulder and ushered him across the street toward a one-story brick box with the words *Line Port Savings and Loan* etched into the limestone foundation.

"Are you sure you don't want to talk at the bank? Because if it's a loan you're looking for, I can assure you, our interest rates beat every other bank in the area."

"Not today, like I said I'm afraid I've changed my mind. But it was a pleasure to meet you, sir."

"Not so hasty, son."

Bart caught a quick flash out of the corner of his eye.

Like sunlight reflected on nickel plating.

Betty pressed up against both of them from behind, and her whisper was harsh in Bart's ear. "It's a loan, alright, boys. And you're going to deliver it to me, smooth and easy." She jabbed her gun into Bart's side. "Just walk nice and natural into the bank."

For his part, Dierking was suitably surprised. "What goes on here? Miss Cooper? What's the meaning of this assault?"

Bart caught himself breathing a sigh of relief. He had hoped Dierking wasn't involved in the situation, and it was clear from his reaction he wasn't.

"That's not a single shot weapon," Bart said. "That's a Navy revolver."

"I lied," Betty said, with a smirk.

"I'll bet it's not the first time you've lied," Bart said. "For example, when you said you didn't know the gray man back at Stone Creek Station. Or when you said you didn't know my name."

"That's right, Gardner. We know all about you."

"The perfect patsy."

Betty laughed with agreement. "The perfect patsy."

"But did you know I was the boxing champion of my school?"

"Boxing?"

With one fast lunge, Bart lashed out,

knocking Betty's gun from her hand.

Reacting rather quickly for his size, Dierking scooped up the weapon in time for Bart to yell out a warning.

"Behind you," he said.

Dierking spun around, firing the revolver even as the man in the pinstriped suit bore down on him from behind.

The banker's aim was true, and the gray man tumbled backwards to earth with a yelp.

Betty crouched low, backing away with a hiss. "You stupid man. You must know you've condemned your wife and child, Gardner. We didn't lie when we said we'd kill her. Your daughter too."

"I don't think so," Bart said.

Standing over a writhing man and holding a smoking gun, Dierking was the picture of composure, but he wasn't able to hide at least a touch of bewilderment. "What's this all about?"

"A bank robbery, sir," Bart said. "Or rather, you'd give me the bank's money, and these two would rob me later, someplace down one of the lesser-traveled trails on my way to West Camp."

"How much were they thinking I'd be loaning you?"

"Ten-thousand dollars. After you heard

my story, they believed you'd have no choice." Bart pulled the crumpled extortion note from his suit pocket and handed it to Dierking.

"Speculation," Betty said. "You're risking your wife's life."

"Am I? My wife who, even now, might be praying the rosary for me?"

"Exactly."

"My *Methodist* wife, who doesn't know a rosary from a thorn bush."

Her angry reply caught in Betty's throat. "I meant — that is . . ."

"You don't even know her name."

Beside the post office, Brother Daniel shouted out, "All aboard the coach for Pacific, West Camp, and Green Valley."

Bart smoothed out his jacket and pants. "She belongs in jail, Mr. Dierking. I can mail in a formal complaint if need be."

The gray man groaned and tried to sit up, but fell back, the side of his suit coat soaked with blood. Betty ran to him and, kneeling, picked up his hand.

"With this note as evidence, I imagine they'll confess ready enough." Dierking reached for Bart's hand and shook it. "You must be eager to move on."

"Thank you, sir."

"One question. When did you know?"

"Not all at once, and not entirely until I climbed out of the stage just now and saw our pinstriped friend there loitering around in the alley by the bank. But one thing bothered me from the beginning."

"What's that?"

"There's no way for a stage, or even a man on horse, to get from Stone Creek Station to West Camp in six hours. In fact, they never intended me to make West Camp."

"Plus, you caught the haberdashery tags on the hat and parasol."

"That too," Bart agreed.

He turned toward the stage, but before he left, he told Betty, "My wife's name is Louise. And my daughter's name is Tabitha."

"You all live in Green Valley then?" Dierking said.

"No sir," Bart said with a grin. "It just so happens, we live in paradise."

MAKING HAY

The big men argued in front of the saloon's south window, each of them armed with Colt six-shooters, neither of them what barkeep Len Bennet would call patient. Sunday afternoon and inside the Broke Steer it was shadowy and cool, the late summer breeze thick with alfalfa, and heat shimmered up from the fresh cut field outside. Len polished a couple mugs for the third or fourth time, just to look busy behind the long walnut counter.

Pretending not to hear the accusations fly.

Trying hard to keep his stomach from tying in knots.

"You're lying to me, Chet," said Sanford Block.

Chet Warner fired back, "Like hell."

The last thing Len wanted to see inside his young Bloomtown business was a fight.

Sandy was the village sheriff, six feet and some odd inches of gristle and cow dust wearing a long-sleeved cotton shirt, leather vest, and jeans. Before a scrap of tin got pinned on his chest, Sandy had been foreman on the last road grade to climb the mountain, then ramrod for the Circle K — tough as any cattleman you'd find this side of the Missouri.

His gun rig was custom-tooled leather with a series of flourishes and a rosette stamped on either side of his bullet loops. And the supple holster was stitched with an embossed five-pointed star.

Mighty damned expensive. But cowmen made good money in Nebraska.

Sandy's Colt had mahogany smooth grips.

Len watched the lawman poke an iron finger into Chet Warner's chest and seethe under his steel breath.

"You'll give me the truth, or I'll pound it out of you."

Len flinched at Sandy's choice of words, glancing over his shoulders at his polished yard-long mirror and wall full of sparkling glass bottles, most of them at least half full.

The Broke Steer couldn't afford to host much of a tussle. The bills were still unpaid from the last brawl to sweep through the place, and after his wife took him for all he was worth, Len needed to make do for a while with the inventory he had.

Push come to shove, he could tap one of the wealthy ranchers in the valley. But he hated to do that again. He'd gone to that well one time too many already.

Red-faced and puffy, Chet let his liver spot–speckled hand drop to his waistline. His fingers brushed the ivory butt at his holster. "You wanna pound something, Sheriff? You can always pound sand."

Sandy's gnarled fist matched Chet's at the level of the gun. "Tell me the truth about Ernie, and we won't either one of us have to pound anything," he said.

Both men let their fingers hover above their guns.

Len put a mug down lightly on the bar and tossed the white towel over his shoulder. When he spoke, he did his best not to stammer.

"Y-you boys wouldn't w-wanna take your disagreement outside . . . would you?"

Sandy and Chet held each other's gaze with grim determination. Without dropping his attention, Sandy answered first. "I wouldn't want that at all," he said. He cocked his high Stetson hat toward the window and the sunbaked stubble field outside. "Hotter'n the devil out there. Bad enough young Ernie's gotta suffer. Be danged if I'll put myself into a stroke."

"You ain't half the man Ernie Monks is, Sheriff," said Chet. "And him being just a boy."

Just as well they'd get back to talking about the kid, thought Len.

It was Ernie Monks they were arguing about.

Len watched through the window, saw the farm boy traipse across the hayfield, a shirt-less string bean with drooping old corduroy pants and heavy boots. Practiced motion swept his three-tined fork under tufts of drying green hay and shoulders burnt golden-brown launched them into small piles.

Small piles became medium piles, and Ernie made medium piles into mountains.

Making hay was about all he was good for, thought Len.

Kid was the village idiot, and Sandy wanted him for some kind of crime.

Len wasn't real clear on the details.

"Tell me where Ernie was last night," said the sheriff. He took a step toward Chet, his spurs jingling on the rough-cut wood floor. "He works for you. You ought to know."

For his part, Chet still wasn't having it. The farmer wasn't as muscled as Sandy, but he had two inches on the lawman. And outweighed him too, though all of it was flab.

Watching Chet's fleshy jowls turn red with the strain of anger, Len thought a sodbuster ought to be in better shape. But naturally the old cus had Ernie doing most of his farm work.

Just like today.

Chet puffed up his chest and stood up to the sheriff.

"Ernie was taking supper with me," said Chet. "Right here at the Steer. Afterwards, we sat outside on the boardwalk for about an hour. Just ask Len if you don't believe me."

Sandy whipped around like a cat after a barn sparrow, "Is that right, barkeep?" Voice hissing like a hot copper kettle.

"What's that?" said Len, pretending again. He'd learned long ago not to reveal too much, and he wasn't about to admit he'd been eavesdropping.

Not that you could ignore them. Anybody in the saloon could follow the conversation clear as the August air.

Not that there was anybody else in there. Sunday afternoon, the place was empty except for the three men.

"Did Mr. Warner and Ernie take supper here last night?" said Sandy.

Put on the spot, Len was glad they were alone.

There was nobody in the room to witness him siding with a farmer.

"As a matter of fact, they were, Sheriff." But then Len decided to add something. "Of course, I don't recall them sitting outside once't they'd left the table."

In fact, he did — but decided he didn't owe the sodbusters a damn thing and didn't particularly want to help.

Sandy's lip twitched at the revelation. "That's your story?"

Len said it was. After all, it wasn't a full and complete lie. The two had supped on biscuits and gravy with fresh corn on the cob directly under the south window. "That's the truth."

"Who made the supper?" said Sandy.

"Excuse me?"

"Wondered who made the supper," reiterated the sheriff. "Since your wife's moved away, I mean."

Len cleared his throat with surprise. Though he had no reason to be startled. News spread through Bloomtown like hayseed, especially bad news when the grangers' wives got together at the market.

It had been a full two days, and everybody in town likely knew Clara was gone.

"I made supper myself," said Len. "I'm a fine cook in my own right."

"Biscuits and beef gravy," said Sandy. "Sweet corn on the cob. Sounds like quite a fine meal." His lips stretched into a satisfied smile. "Wish I could get me some sweet corn. Where'd you get yours?"

"Mr. Higgins," said Len. "Over at the market."

Sandy nodded. "Out of curiosity, sir," he said, "where'd she go?"

"Where'd she go?"

"Your wife."

"Oh, Clara. You want to know where she went?"

"Are we done here?" said Chet Warner, tipping back his battered old cap to wipe sweat from his forehead. "Ernie's gettin' finished up out there."

"No, we ain't done," said Sandy. He hooked a chair leg with the toe of his boot and jerked it out. "Take a load off," he said, indicating the seat.

Then he turned back to Len. "I apologize, Mr. Bennet. Ain't none of my business."

Len smiled and waved off the comment. "Think nothing of it."

"It's just with this here shooting thing, I forgot myself."

Len felt like he'd been slapped with a cold

dishrag. "Sh-shooting?" he said.

Sandy nodded. "That's what I'm talkin' to Mr. Warner about."

Chet settled down into the chair Sandy had offered. Tossing his thumb toward the open window and the field beyond, he said, "Sheriff thinks Ernie done it."

"Done what?" said Len.

"Killed a woman in cold blood."

Len's stomach fell to his shoes. He failed to hold back his stutter. "Killed? Wh-who i-is she?"

Sandy wagged his head back and forth before he shrugged. "No way to know," he said. "Shotgun blast to the face. The poor lamb is unrecognizable."

"Sh-shotgun?" Len again thought of his inventory. This time he reached out for an amber bottle.

Procuring three short tumblers, he poured a healthy shot into each before picking up the middle offering and bringing it to his lips. "You boys help yourself. It's on the house."

"Don't mind if I do," said Chet, hauling himself up and over to the bar.

"A shooting," said Len again, his heart pounding. "Good heavens."

"Yeah, the way I've got it pegged, it can't be anybody but Ernie. Happened out near

Chet's place. You know Ernie stays out there."

"It's got nothing to do with us," said Chet.

Outside, Ernie was scooping up the wind rows and folding them into tall, fluffy stacks. Len didn't envy the boy, felt the liquor work on his nerves, felt the trembling inside subside, heard his stutter fade when he said, "The poor boy."

The perfect scapegoat.

"Anything I can do to help?" said Len.

"You've helped some already," said Sandy.

Len couldn't help but notice the men hadn't touched their whiskey. "Drink up, gentlemen. Like I said, it's on me."

Chet shook his head. "I never drink on an empty stomach." Then he said, "Speaking of — what'cha got on the menu tonight, Len?" He gave Sandy a sidelong glance. "Maybe we get the sheriff here some sweet corn, he'd lay off his wild stories about Ernie."

"I got biscuits again. Bacon."

"Nothing from the garden?"

"Cucumbers," said Len.

"Cucumbers," said Chet. "You hear that, Sheriff?"

Sandy nodded. "I did."

"You boys like cucumbers?" said Len.

"I like 'em fine," said Chet.

Sandy scratched the back of his neck. "Wonder if you'd do me a favor, Mr. Bennet?"

"I will if I can."

"Go out there and ask Ernie to step inside here. Don't tell him I asked. Just make up some reason to get him inside."

"You gonna take him in for the shooting of this woman? Whoever she is?"

Sandy pursed his lips but didn't say anything.

It was answer enough.

This time Len made a show about looking over his inventory. The last thing he needed was for Ernie to resist arrest. For the three of them to get into a shootin' match.

"I'll go get him," said Len. "But I'll meet you on the boardwalk out front."

"Fair enough," said Sandy.

Strangely enough, Chet Warner didn't object.

Strolling across the hayfield, the bright afternoon sun a welcome respite from too much time holed up inside the saloon. He needed to get outside more often. Maybe start up a garden of his own. There was still time. Summer wasn't yet too far gone.

Or maybe it was.

Ernie had piled up a lot of hay. And the stubble was awfully yellow and dry.

The stack the kid waited beside was tall as three men and big around as a ring of Conestoga schooners. "Circle the wagons," he said out loud, and laughed.

Because that's what he and Sandy and Chet were gonna do with Ernie. Surround him.

"Ernie?" Len said as he approached the boy. "Sheriff asked me to come get you. Something he wants to talk to you about."

They stood four feet apart. Len in the middle of the hayfield, the white woolen towel still draped over his shoulder. Ernie, shirtless, with drooping corduroy pants and a tin star pinned to the side pocket.

Tin star? He read the legend embossed there.

"Deputy?"

Ernie reached into the haystack beside him and withdrew a lever-action carbine. He pointed it at Len, and without a word nodded back toward the Broke Steer.

Len turned around to see Chet Warner and Sandy Block coming toward him.

Sandy had Len's shotgun in a cradle carry across his arms.

"Nice piece of weaponry you keep under the bar," he said.

"Thought we ought to pick you up out here," said Chet. "Just so's your inventory wouldn't get damaged in the shooting."

"Pick *me* up?" said Len.

"For shooting your wife over at Mulligan's corn patch."

"Good old Mrs. Mulligan," said Chet, smiling at his friend, the sheriff. "Did you know she's the only lady left around town with any sweet corn?"

Sandy nodded.

Len didn't know. "Is that a fact?"

"Damned weevils," said Chet. "Contrary to what you said about Mr. Higgins at the market, he hasn't had any corn in more than a week. Mulligan's always been lucky that way, though. Of course, she told me last night a bunch of her corn had just went missing."

"Cucumbers too," said the sheriff.

Chet shook his head. "Funny that."

Sandy nodded at Ernie. "How about you and Chet go ahead and take Mr. Bennet over to the jail, son? Lock him up good and tight. If he gives you any trouble, you have my permission to shoot him."

Len looked into Ernie's disciplined features and swallowed hard. "I won't give you any trouble," he said.

"Didn't think you would," said Sandy.

205

"Oh, and Ernie? When you get Mr. Bennet locked up, come on over to the bar. Drinks are on him. He said so earlier."

"Mr. Bennet has been a great help to us today," said Chet.

Sandy slapped his friend on the back. "A man's gotta make hay while the sun shines. Ain't that what you sodbusters always say?"

"It is indeed," said Chet.

A Requiem for Byron

Bereft of my youthly idealism after the war betwixt the states and minus any accrued financial resources, I found myself behind a desk in the summer of 1875 mentally copulating with the ponderous sweet prose of young Algot Carlson.

Ah, precious Algot, a master baiter of reluctant words, he possessed the uncanny skill of coaxing a perspiration thin anecdote into a thick as honey narrative, leaving the reader's mind silent and still.

I reveled in his literary ability if not his penmanship.

With the golden glow of sunrise gracing my window, I made check marks on his paper next to the obvious clichés. For Algot, all was fair in love and war. He was, after all, *head over heels* in love, but rest assured — he assured us — *time would heal all wounds.*

The boy had a heart-shaped appreciation

for all things trite and mundane.

And yet there was the quick wit of the Bard about him. The promise of a Keats, if only I could put my finger on it.

I let my attention be drawn by the bird-song outside my window, the final tremolo of the field sparrow, its call starting strong, receding like a penny drop. The Wyoming range, marred only by a single structure, inspired vast contemplation — the delicate perfume of blooming wildflower and sage suggested the tenuous nature of life.

What hidden talents might any of us possess? Who knows when and where they might become manifest? A right turn, the wrong execution, who knows what position we'd achieve?

Young Algot had the makings of a Byron. Who except I would discover it?

Turning back to the composition, I studied Algot's structure, admired his sentences. His declarative phrases were bold, his confessions absolute. Here was not the usual obfuscation, soft and doughy, but instead a bold, resolute admission.

His prepositional phrases offered concrete relationships to objects and other characters.

His narrative pacing was dead-on.

His descriptions were vivid, especially when it came to coitus and killing, subject matter the young writer naturally shies away from.

Finished with the essay, I dropped back in my hardwood chair catching my breath, marveling at the talent of Algot Carlson, wondering how fate allowed me to discover such a gem.

Dare I say *a diamond in the rough.*

But perhaps such common indulgence of my own is the reason I never rose in the ranks at university, instead dropping away, settling for a job in the American West.

Removing my pocket watch, I took in the time.

Nodded to myself.

I put the watch back in my vest, beneath the tin star with its spear-like edges, its razor-sharp responsibilities.

Outside, the sun floated just above the far horizon, behind the wood scaffold where the hangman marched Algot Carlson to his death.

I carried the boy's last confession to the window, held it to my chest as the black hood was fitted, the lever tipped, the boy dropped.

Somewhere the field sparrow sang.

THE PROMISE OF SUMMERLAND

I can still see Catherine's nose wrinkle during that summer of 1885. She had sniffed the lamb-stuffed cabbage roll, then tentatively put it to her lips. I can see her brushing away a glittering strand of blonde from the graceful line of her chin as she took a bite. *Kohlrouladen* grandma called it. From the old country. A staple food in the Bosch home, as regular as mashed potatoes and sourdough bread.

Catherine chewed with delicate precision, her expression showing surprise.

A second bite, and the clean, milk-smooth face registered joyful revelation. She pushed the rest of the roll into her mouth and sucked her fingers clean. "Now you," she said, urging me on with her thick, accented speech.

In Summerland, magic ran wild, and the proof was in nine-year-old Catherine's eyes.

One bite, and the Danish *aebelskivers*

would contribute to the neighborhood melting pot, like the German food before it.

Eyeing the sugar-covered ball of fried dough, I panicked. I was nine, too. And doing something wrong.

"It ain't right," I said out loud without meaning to. "Mama Bosch won't like it."

If we got caught . . .

Catherine said, "Leo, that aebelskiver is for you. Your mama don't have to eat it, and my mama will never know."

Which was more or less how the whole thing began — the two mamas' pride.

On both sides of Summerland Bridge.

A month before Catherine came to the rolling hills of northeast Nebraska, I kept a wood box in a damp sod hidey-hole at Summerland Bridge and spent all my spare time there with it. Mama worried I would leave her for this second home, but of course it was nothing like the frame house on the hill my pa and da onkles built.

But I filled that little wood box with treasures.

Smooth, rainbow-colored rocks. A rusted nose ring from Herman Schulz's bull. A Ponca Indian necklace I placed on a small bed of quilt batting pilfered from Mama's sewing basket. Magic talismans filled with the power of summer against winter. Sunshine against the dark.

In spite of my Lutheran Sunday school education, when I found a tiny bird point arrowhead sticking out of the riverbank, I kept it in my pocket at all times to ward off evil during afternoon adventures in the river bluffs.

At first, I wondered if it worked, but a week after I started carting my arrowhead around, a girl appeared out of nowhere in the lower cow pasture.

Good luck? Or was it bad?

She wasn't just any girl.

I was alone in the crick bed under the bridge, a stone's throw from my magic box and pitching dirt clods into the stagnant runoff, when she came to the edge of the bridge and said, "Hello."

Like she was an *American.*

But with a heavy accent.

After I said, "Hi" back to her, she piled on a load of gibberish. "Mit navn er Catherine. Hvem er du?"

I sorted through all her chattering as best I could and finally said "Mein name ist Leo," just to show her I could talk foreign, too.

My introduction set her back a step because she didn't know Mama and Pa came from Schleswig-Holstein. At home we all spoke German.

My words weren't enough to scare her off though, and pretty soon Catherine pulled her dress down over her knees and sat down in the grass. She let her bare feet dangle over the creek bank.

I almost tossed a clod at her.

"Ich rede nicht mit Danen," I said.

I don't talk to Danes.

Which wasn't exactly true, because there was Nord Svensen who rode past our place on his way to the other Lutheran church on Sundays. Whenever we saw him, we all raised our hands and said hello. But that was it. Mama never let us say any more on account of the old country war. And Danes smelling funny. And having lice in their hair. And everything else.

I had to squint looking at Catherine because the sun was right behind her head, like a halo.

If she had bugs that day, I never knew because I didn't get close enough to see.

When she came to Summerland later on, I forgot to check.

That first day, it was me who ran off like a skeered rabbit, but when she showed up a few days later, I stood my ground.

By now I'd heard from Pa that the Sørensen family had struck a claim across the bunchgrass from us, so my crick hide-away was a kind of fence or boundary line.

A bunch of Danes wasn't about to chase me away from my magic spot.

Already on the second day, Catherine carried a round iron fry pan with a lid. When I crawled out into the sunshine, she came down bold as a newborn calf, and talking English, said, "Here. For you to eat."

I kept quiet and gave her the stink eye as she put the fry pan down on the ground between us.

After a while, she got tired of looking at me, and scurried away across the meadow for home, leaving the covered pan behind. I wondered about those bare feet, soles black with Nebraska hardpan. Didn't Danes wear any shoes?

I asked Mama about it when I delivered the fry pan. Mama knows just about everything there is to know about Danes.

But instead of answering my question, she sat there staring at the fry pan.

The whole time I talked to her, neither of us had dared open it.

When Pa asked about it later, Mama lifted her chin.

"Der abfall."

Garbage.

I was duty bound then to carry the pan

outside to where the cats gathered hoping to cash in on a few scraps after dinner. I picked up the iron lid and turned the heavy thing upside down.

Nothing came out.

And then I saw the fry pan was a special one, like a cast-iron egg carton with depressions filled with round, fluffy pastries. Golden brown and sugar coated, they clung to the interior iron of the pan until I popped them loose with my fingers.

"Aebelskivers," Mama said, shaking her head behind me, and the hungry cats pounced.

Within the hour, pride forced her into making a dozen cabbage rolls.

Stuffed with lamb, pepper, cumin, and wrapped in cooked cabbage, the finished Kohlrouladen stayed in the root cellar overnight.

Next day, I was volunteered by Mama to carry the tin pan of rolls over to the Sørensen place.

"We are as Christian as they are," Mama said, with a haughty tone. "No Danish hausfrau will have the chance to put her nose in the air around the Bosch family. We will give as good as we get — and more."

For my part, I gave as good as a mile walk, carrying both pans to Summerland Bridge, before pooping out in the heat of the afternoon.

Before long, Catherine showed up, and we sat in the shade of the bridge together. I was glad I didn't have to walk all the way to her house. But still annoyed at the presence of a girl in my special place.

"Here," I said, shoving the tin pan offering under her chin.

"What is it?"

"You ain't the only ones who have food." Then I gave her back the aebelskivers pan.

She nodded at the empty pan. "Good, da?" Meaning the sugary dough balls.

I shrugged, embarrassed to tell her the truth. The way the cats ate, I guess the food must have been good. It wasn't entirely a lie when I said, "Da."

That was our third time together, and she already had me talking like her — whether I knew it or not.

"I have to go," I said. "Your ma can keep the pan. We don't need it back."

Such generosity seemed unheard of. Catherine shook her head. "No, Leo. It is yours."

"Keep it if you want."

She peeked under the lid at the cabbage. "Is good?"

"Cabbage and meat. It's good."

From the face she made, I could tell she

was disappointed.

I said, "Did you expect candy or something?"

"Oh. No."

"It's okay if you did."

"I will enjoy the . . . what?"

"German Kohlrouladen. Cabbage and meat."

She walked away backwards. "Bye, Leo."

I wished she would stay, but I wasn't going to tell her that.

Anyway, she came back the next day.

The cabbage empty, the aebelskivers pan full.

I was reluctant to accept the big fry pan. You can spoil a passel of barn cats only so far.

"You must take it," Catherine said. I recognized her appeal. Not only would it be rude to turn down the gift of aebelskivers, but Catherine would be in trouble. And strangely enough, I didn't want her to be in trouble.

"Did you like the cabbage?" I said.

"Oh," she said, like the question surprised her. "Da. Very much." A lie if I'd ever heard one. Her ma had dumped out the food. Same as mine.

"Thank you for these able-skeeters," I said.

She corrected me. "*Aebelskivers.* Like . . . uh . . . pancake ball?"

"Pancake ball."

That night, Mama tossed 'em to the cats.

The next day was Sunday with church, and then on Monday Pa drove me in to Niobrara City to buy shoes. By Tuesday morning, Mama had a task for me.

She dropped the square tin pan full of Kohlrouladen into my hands. "To take to the Sørensen's."

I wondered out loud. "Maybe they don't want any more?"

"Hush," Mama said. "We have been poor neighbors, keeping their aebelskivers pan for nearly a week." Her voice was rich with charity. "What if they only have the one pan? If it were me, I would be upset with a neighbor who kept my only pan."

In Mama's way of thinking, more cabbage rolls were due penance for such a grievous crime.

The fact is, when I set out for Summerland, I had no intention of eating the peace offering I carried on top of the aebelskivers pan like a lit box of powder. But the day was pleasant with a cool breeze, and my breakfast had burned away by the time I got to the bridge.

218

Hunkering down into a shady patch of grass, I removed the lid from Mama's pan and finished one of the cabbage rolls in two bites, savoring the spicy lamb, still warm, and the strong tang of the cabbage.

I might have eaten them all if Catherine hadn't arrived then, a second aebelskivers pan held in both hands.

"I brought your other pan back."

Embarrassed, she said, "I . . . forgot yours." Mama would be pleased by Catherine's forgetfulness.

She'd be one up on the game.

I couldn't help but feel bad.

Even to my nine-year-old reasoning, the whole exchange was ridiculous. Here we were, two kids who should've been swimming in the river, or exploring a cave, or hiking up Maiden's Leap — and instead, we were peaceful negotiators for a war that took place years before and thousands of miles away.

I thought about Mama feeding our barn cats with Sørensen bread, and I couldn't stop the confession that rose to my lips. "We didn't eat the aebelskivers. Mama says they're garbage."

Expecting the worst, my spontaneous betrayal had the opposite effect.

Instead of crying or yelling or cursing at

me in her crazy language, Catherine's face lightened. Her cheeks flushed, and the corner of her mouth came up in a smile. "I will tell you a secret," she said, but I finished it for her.

"Your ma threw out the cabbage rolls?"

"Da," Catherine said. "She has not allowed us to eat them."

I looked down at the pan of Kohlrouladen I carried.

Catherine looked at the fresh helping of aebelskivers.

"I don't know what you think," I said. "But I think we have the makings of a fine lunch."

She swallowed her first cabbage roll with relish.

But at the last minute I hesitated.

"It ain't right," I said out loud without meaning to. "Mama Bosch won't like it."

Catherine said, "Leo, your mama don't have to eat it."

She was right of course. But I had to figure it out.

"Catherine, what was the Second Schleswig War about?"

At home, I had heard it called John's War, for my lost uncle. And William's War for the other brother killed. And I knew the Danes started it because they were pigheaded and selfish.

"I don't know," Catherine said. "It was before I was born."

"It was before my family came here," I told her.

"It was long before we came here."

Sugar on my fingers, I brought the aebelskivers to my lips. "The grown-ups can have their wars," I said. "I will eat their pancake balls."

"And I will eat their cabbage."

"When we grow up," I said, chewing the wonderfully rich, warm Danish delicacy, "I won't throw away food."

"And we won't have any wars."

"And even if we talk other languages, we'll all be friends. Da?"

I can still see Catherine's nose wrinkle that summer of 1885.

"Da," she said, laughing, and the magic of Summerland and my arrowhead and all my lucky charms promised it would happen just like we imagined.

THE LIVELIHOOD OF JEREMIAH TEAGUE

Tom Carpenter leaned on a broom in the doorway of his west Texas mercantile to get a better view as the circus wagon rolled into town pulled by a snorting quartet of cinder-black mares with ember bright eyes.

At least it looked like a circus wagon.

At first.

A modified Concord stagecoach with a slender man at the helm, its wood sides washed in forest green and emblazoned with orange and yellow swirls of the brush with brass rails atop and crimson-spoked wheels below. The horses wheeled the coach through a cloud of dust and the driver braked at a rakish angle in the middle of main street Perdition. It all came to a rocking stop smack-dab between the boardwalks of Sheriff John's jail and the Leadbelly Saloon, and the man with the four-in-hand dropped his laces. Stood. Took a bow.

And announced himself.

"Greetings one, greetings all, your humble servant, Jeremiah Teague requests your brief attention." Teague cleared his throat. "That is, if you value the safety of your family and well-being of your homes."

Tom shook his head with amusement. Another damn peddler.

Next door, Clem Jarret, the barber, stuck his bald pate through the open window of his shop.

"What do you suppose this one's selling?"

Tom chuckled at the barber's friendly comradery. "Probably the same as most of the others."

Jeremiah Teague restated his plea for attention and pulled a bouquet of flowers from his coat.

"Sometimes it smells better," Tom said.

"But it's the same old —"

The barber's opinion was cut off by the happy squeal of four merry moppets encircling the wagon.

Tom leaned his broom against the jamb and took two steps out onto the boardwalk.

"Suffer not the good children to come unto me," Teague said. With a deft hand he plucked a blossom for each of the four from his collection.

"Come one, come all, is the standard rally cry," said Jeremiah Teague tipping back his lavender stovepipe hat. "But truly, my spiel is only for those hale and hearty folks responsible for the common good of Perdition."

Lowering his chin, he allowed his ebony whiskers to brush his scarlet string tie. From under a lowered brow, he moved his gaze to Tom and the barber, to the parasol-equipped pedestrian in the street, the Widow Hemmings. "Those men or women who value justice."

Tom walked into the dusty street to get a better look at the colorful drummer.

Jeremiah Teague was selling something. But what?

Jarret came out of his barbershop, and Sam Wilkes joined him from the saloon with Abigail Bingham. The Widow Hemmings swirled her parasol and clutched her purse but didn't turn away. Sheriff John appeared at his office door with his deputy, a red-haired gent named Sykes.

Along with his peers, Tom cupped his chin with a finger and took the tall fellow's measure.

"What is it you're selling, Teague?"

"Ah-ha!" Teague turned his full attention to Tom and tossed the remainder of his flowers to one of the little girls. "I can always tell a man of character. A man of strength. A leader in the community." Teague bent slightly in the middle and took in the tall false front of Tom's mercantile building. "Is this your store?"

Even at a distance, Teague smelled of cheap whiskey. A second look at his flamboyant attire — the purple claw hammer coat, the striped trousers, the gold watch fob — all showed signs of neglect. The clothes were new, but Teague was unkempt.

When Tom didn't answer, Sheriff John took center stage. "What can we do for you, Mr. Teague? You said something about justice?"

"Yes, indeed, Sheriff. Yes, indeed. You might say justice is just what I'm selling." Teague had a lazy eye that lingered on Tom even as he turned his attention to John.

"If it's guns you're peddling, we've got enough —"

"Oh, no, Sheriff. No, no. It's not guns I trade in."

"Then what?"

"The truth, sir. I trade in the truth."

By now, a healthy circle of potential customers had gathered on the boardwalks of Perdition, and the curious people of the town advanced with not a little delight. Entertainments, after all, were few and far between in this part of the panhandle.

The barkeep, Sam Wilkes, asked the question on everybody's mind. "How, exactly, does a man peddle the truth?"

Teague turned to Wilkes but reserved his answer until after he'd gazed a heartbeat too long at Abigail Bingham in her tight corset and satin working girls' dress. "Don't you have the loveliest yellow hair, ma'am? So fresh, so . . . dare I say? Clean."

Abigail peered through heavily made-up eyes. "Beg y'r pardon?"

"Would that your hands would likewise be so clean?"

"What about my hands?"

"Hey, you oughtn't to say nothing about my Abby's hands," Wilkes said.

"There, there, my good man. Don't take offense." Teague swirled around with a pattern of fancy footwork, raising the dust in the street and trailing the tails of his coat. "How many of us have truly clean hands? Oh, I don't mean free of dirt, cleansed of the routine dust and chaff of the day's work. I mean clean as in free of sin?"

"I still don't like what you're implying about Abby," said Wilkes.

"That makes one of us, sir." Teague's eyebrows wagged up and down. "That makes one of us."

The Widow Hemmings gasped and almost

dropped her parasol.

Before anybody else could take offense at his language, Teague danced a jig and removed two glass blob bottles of liquid from the inside pockets of his coat. "People of Perdition, may I present the Truth." He held both bottles high at arm's length. "And the Truth shall set you free."

Within seconds, a three-legged folding table appeared from inside the wagon, and Teague spread a blue, fringed satin cloth over it. Half a dozen bottles of Truth appeared with fast sleight of hand.

Just like that, "We're in business, folks." Teague doffed his hat toward the ladies.

Tom Carpenter believed he was missing something and joined Teague at the display. "Thus far, you've done nothing but speak in riddles, Mr. Teague. You talk about justice and truth. But you're selling bottles of what appears to be water."

"Ah, friend," Teague said, picking up a bottle. "So much more than water."

Tom held the compact, narrow bottle in hand. The clear liquid beneath the stopper looked for all the world like water, and only two or three good swallows at that. "Is this for drinking?"

Teague snatched back the sample. "Not for drinking! Never, never drink of Truth."

He moved the bottle into the widow's hands where she held it at arm's length. "Rather, cleanse your souls. Cleanse your hands. The truth will out."

"It's for hand washing? A kind of soap?" said the barber Jarret.

"Oh it's much more than mere soap. Jeremiah Teague's patented Truth cleanses the soul by revealing sin." Again, he turned to the widow. "Ma'am, if you would do me the honor of uncorking that bottle and splashing a few dollops of Truth onto my hands? Take some for yourself as well."

"Oh, I'd rather not."

"Please, ma'am. Don't be shy."

"Well . . ."

"It's perfectly safe, my dear."

"If I must," said the Widow Hemmings. She was a prim and proper lady, but she'd been a schoolteacher at an early age. She could roll up her sleeves with the best of them.

The liquid poured out on Teague's hands and he held them up high, dripping, and "Clean," he proclaimed. The Widow did the same.

"Hey, what are you trying to pull?" said Sam Wilkes. "That's nothing but water on your hands."

Teague waved his spotless hands in the air

to dry, then invited Sam to come closer. "I admit it looks like water, but Truth is much more. For some . . . like me," and then he indicated the widow, "and I'm sure, the lovely lady here, a helping of Truth is simply a good way to wash away the day's work." The Widow Hemmings handed back the half-full bottle of liquid.

When Teague turned back to Wilkes, his manner changed. Now his voice was tinged with something else.

Judgment.

"For others, Truth . . . reveals."

Tom Carpenter watched as Teague quickly snatched up the barkeep's hands and without asking splashed out a helping of his elixir.

Nothing happened at first.

Like Teague's previous demonstration, the watery bath dripped from Wilke's hands clear and clean. But then something happened. The drops grew thick, dark. The splotches left on the dusty street were crimson red, like blood.

Wilkes stepped back and held his wet hands up in front of his face.

Before the entire town, the skin of his hands appeared to swirl and grow cloudy with a scarlet foam. "What the heck?" He shook the dew from his fingers, a blood-red stain, growing . . . growing.

"What did you do?"

The crowd reacted with a collective gasp, but Teague reassured them. "The process is entirely painless, my friends. My Truth isn't about punishment. It's about revelation."

Now Wilkes's scarlet hands were almost entirely covered with the vibrant stain.

Deputy Sheriff Sykes said. "What's all this prove, Teague?"

"You've heard the phrase, 'caught red-handed'?"

"I ain't done nothing wrong," said Wilkes. He rubbed frantically at his hands, but the red stain wouldn't come off.

"The Truth says otherwise."

Sykes followed up. "You're saying this juice of yours is some kind of . . . crime detector?"

"Not so much crime . . . as sin."

Teague's smile was too smug for Tom. Too pompous. He enjoyed the trick just a little bit too much. "Sam Wilkes is a good man," Tom said.

"I'm sure he is," said Teague. "Part of the time. But we all live in the balance, sir. And my Truth will show where the scales come down most often. Somebody like myself, or the Widow here, can wash their hands with a clear conscience, and similar skin. Unfortunately for others . . ."

Teague held the remains of the bottle out toward Abigail, the Leadbelly Saloon girl. "Would you care to try it, sister?"

"You rotten son of a —"

"I'll try it," said a voice from the crowd.

Tom turned to watch his neighbor, Clem Jarret, step forward.

"Way I figure it, a barber can't have too many tonics. And if this one will keep my patrons honest . . ."

Teague held up a finger. "It won't keep them honest, sir. But it will show you who's who and what's what. Sometimes simply by way of who's willing to partake of it." Teague kept his lazy eye on Abigail. "And who's not."

"I don't think that's a fair way to judge folks," said Tom.

Teague scoffed at him. "And what . . . exactly, do you have to hide, sir?"

Jarret looked around the crowd. In his eggshell white shirt, black trousers, braces, and clean-shaven chin, he was the Everyman face of Perdition. The look he offered Tom was one of empathy, but when he turned to Wilkes there was no love lost.

"I can personally testify that Mr. Wilkes cheated me half a dollar on his barber bill last month. I've carried him twice as long as

I ought, with nary a word when I can expect payback."

Wilkes screwed up his face with anger. Tom thought he saw shame creeping in there too. Behind the eyes. Behind the stammering voice. "Dad-blam it, I . . . I been meaning to pay you."

Teague roared with triumph. "You see, friends? You see how my Truth is the tonic this town needs to set its people right?"

Jarret handed over his two bits in exchange for a fresh bottle of Truth. Immediately he opened the stopper and handed the bottle over to Tom. "Pour some out, won't you?"

Tom spilled a healthy dose onto the barber's hands. Rubbing vigorously, he encouraged another dose. Several seconds went past. A minute. Then two.

The barber's hands were clean.

"Why not share some with your neighbor?" suggested Teague. Jarret retrieved the bottle from Tom and held it up to the crowd.

Abigail spoke up. "How do we know every second dose isn't the red one?"

The sheriff agreed. "It could be a trick that way."

Teague stepped to the side and hooked a curly-topped moppet away from his herd of children. "I assure you, there's no trick. Try

232

it out on this young man here, why don't you?"

"I shouldn't think a child needs your kind of right and wrong, Teague." Tom said.

"But a child is nothing if not innocent," said Teague. He nodded at Jarret: *Go ahead.*

The little boy held up his hands. The barber dribbled some Truth into them.

"Rub it around, son. Rub it around and hold up your hands."

The boy followed Teague's instructions and lifted his palms for all to see.

Clean.

"I'll take a bottle," said Deputy Sykes. Sheriff John gave him a dirty look, but Sykes said, "I can't see why it wouldn't help in our line of work."

"Why, naturally, son. Naturally. Truth helps in all lines of work. And all areas of life." Teague offered him the bottle he'd just used on the kid. "Help yourself to the remainder of this sample." His voice fell into a musical patter, almost like a preacher, Tom thought.

"Husbands offer some to wives. Wives to husbands. Parents to children. Children to your friends." Teague patted the curly boy on his head. "Everybody should live by the Truth."

Deputy Sykes dumped the rest of the

sample onto his hands.

Almost immediately a series of whirling red blobs began to form.

"Hold on, here. What gives?"

Teague clucked his tongue at the deputy and smiled knowingly at the crowd. "I'm sure some of you aren't surprised."

"I should say not," said the Widow Hemmings. "I saw Mr. Sykes with Miss Abigail after hours just last week."

Sykes protested, his scarlet palms held out flat. "I was watching out for her. Just walking her home after work."

"He was walking me home after work," Abigail said.

"If that's so, why not wash your hands in Truth and prove it?" the Widow said. Then she held out two coins. "I'll take two bottles, Mr. Teague."

"Of course, my dear."

"I'll take some, too," said an old man on the edge of the crowd.

"A wise choice," Teague said.

"A bottle here," came the cry from behind him.

The mother of the boy said, "Two bottles for me, please."

The crowd pressed in close, herding Tom back up onto the boardwalk in front of his store. Jarret and the Widow were in the middle of it. True converts to the cause, along with the little boy and his mother.

Back in front of the saloon was Miss Abigail, supplying bar rags to Sam Wilkes and Deputy Sykes. The red stains on their hands didn't seem to be coming off. Even as Tom watched, a man strolled out of the saloon to brush past them.

"I'll take a bottle of Truth."

A well-dressed lady joined him. "Pass it back this way."

Before long, it seemed like everybody in Perdition was buying a bottle of Teague's stuff.

And just as soon as they'd paid, they were trying it out.

On themselves, and on each other.

"I knew it! I knew it all the time," screamed a middle-aged woman at her husband, his hands a ruddy crimson. "I should never have trusted you."

"Aw, but Stella . . ."

"I'm free," came another loud holler. "Free from sin, free of the devil." The town drunk, Ebenezer Jacks, held up clean hands drenched with Truth.

Tom caught Sam Wilkes's questioning glance. If any man was full of sin, it was Ebenezer.

The irony wasn't lost on Teague. "It just

goes to show you," he said. "The verdict of men is often mistaken. Put your faith in the determination of Truth."

The crowd was a whirlwind of laughing and talking, shouting and wild cries. Sheriff John strode forward and cleared a space around Teague and his wagon. "We'll have order here. Order you all."

"Aw, button it up, John," said a voice from the crowd.

"Y'r so damn proud," said another. Then: "I'd like to see what kind of blood is on our sheriff's hands."

"Yeah, let's see Sheriff John wash his hands in Truth."

The three voices came from a trio of brothers who emerged from the crowd. Tom recognized the Delancey boys. Known outlaws who always just managed to escape the hangman's noose. Tom glanced at their palms. Wet or dry, he couldn't tell.

But they were in the clear for now.

"Come on, Sheriff. Let's get them hands wet," said the lead Delancey. He flipped a coin toward Teague and the salesman handed over a bottle.

"I will not," said the sheriff.

The second Delancey pulled a gun from the leather holster on his hip and said, "I think you will."

Tom swallowed hard as the cacophony of the crowd died away. Everybody's focus was on the impromptu trial taking place on the street in front of them.

Guilty or innocent? A good sheriff or corrupt?

A few drops of Truth would tell.

The air was electric.

Sheriff John rolled his eyes and gave out with a sigh. "It's hardly worth holding a gun on me." He held out his hands and Delancey poured.

The crowd held its breath.

And the sheriff's hands turned blood red.

The cry that rose up was equal parts angry and surprised. Outraged, but gleeful. Before John could move, the first Delancey reached for him.

John pulled his own six-shooter and beat a hasty retreat for the saloon as the townspeople turned on him. "He's always been a dirty sheriff," somebody said.

"Just like his deputy."

"Law and order's a joke in Perdition. Always had been."

The crowd's mood was less joyful now, and more maniacally eager. Teague could barely keep up with the swarm of transactions. Tom wondered how much of the odd tonic Teague carried.

And he wondered how it worked.

A different patron of the Leadbelly Saloon limped past Tom as if a burden had been piled on his back. He gazed at his red-stained hands and sobbed. "I don't reckon I understand this." He showed Tom his palms. "I've tried to be a good man. I've really tried."

The man wandered away, back into the wild, flailing crowd.

"Ain't you getting a couple bottles for yourself?"

Tom spun at the voice and saw Clem Jarret near his doorway. He and the barber had always gotten on well. You had to in a West Texas frontier town. You relied on your friends and neighbors to survive. Without friendship, without trust . . . a man — a town — had nothing.

"I reckon I don't have much call for what Mr. Teague is selling," Tom said.

Jarret shook his head. "I can't say I agree with you." He nodded toward the contentious crowd. "Every house needs a good airing out. Every community."

"Red-handed. Literally caught you red-handed."

"Gimme another bottle, Teague."

"You rotten skunk."

Tom gave Jarret a skeptical expression.

"They don't seem too community minded right now, do they?"

"Maybe it's you ain't so community minded," Jarret said. He clutched a bottle of Teague's truth in hand. "Maybe you're afraid of what the contents of this bottle would show about Tom Carpenter's character. About Honest Tom's mercantile shop?"

Tom felt the remark like a slap in the face, but he held his temper.

"I don't know how that juice works, Clem. But it's a trick of some kind. It has to be."

"Why does it have to be? I think it's just what Mr. Teague says it is. You've seen all the advancements of science these days. The railroad. The telegraph. Imagine telling your old grandma you could transmit a message across the country within a few minutes."

Tom gazed out over Perdition's main street. At least three full-fledged knock-down drag-out fights were underway. Beside the post office, two ladies were squabbling over the heads of two children wrestling on the ground below. One of the women had red hands, the other didn't.

"This is different, Clem."

In front of the sheriff's office, a mob of rowdy men were calling on the sheriff and the deputy to turn in their guns and their stars with an angry chant: "Lock 'em up.

Lock 'em up!"

Tom clenched his jaw as Jeremiah Teague made his way out of the boisterous mass of patrons toward the boardwalk. The man was radiant with glee and his pockets bulged with money. "But I'm ever so thirsty," he said. "Could I trouble either of you men for a cup of water?"

Jarret was only too eager to help. "I'll do you one better. The saloon has fresh squeezed lemonade. Would you fancy a cup, sir?"

Teague's smile was genuine. "Indeed, I would. Thank you, kind barber."

Tom watched his friend trot off like a lapdog.

Teague was likewise amused. He turned to Tom and offered him a knowing look.

"You're not too impressed with me, Mr. Carpenter."

"You know my name."

"Not surprised?"

"Not really." He walked into his shop and breathed in the still, sweet air, rich with smells of sawdust and cornmeal. Casually he retrieved his broom and started sweeping. "I figure a man like you studies his mark fairly well before making a play."

Teague followed him inside with a robust laugh. "You wouldn't be wrong," he said.

"Is that how you do it, Teague? You research ahead of time who's good and who's bad? Then roll into town and start passing out judgment?"

"Nothing so well-orchestrated." Teague walked along one of the store's long countertops, dragging his finger as he gazed at the variety of goods Tom carried.

"Coffee, wheat flour, rolled oats," Teague said. "Cast-iron pans. Tin cups. Plates."

"See anything you need?" Tom continued to sweep.

"Given your disposition, I'm not sure you'd want to do business with me."

Tom shrugged. "Your money spends as good as any. I don't have to like a man to do business with him."

"I'm so glad to hear you say so," Teague said. "Because I have a proposition that might be mutually beneficial."

Tom stopped sweeping and leaned on his broom.

From the street, somebody yelled. "Grab hold of that filthy polecat."

And again, the demand, "Lock 'em up."

"What's your proposition, Teague? I'm not in the market for gimmicked water."

"Not water, Mr. Carpenter. It's a chemical that reacts with lye."

"It . . . reacts . . . ?"

241

Teague's smile was wide. He nodded with satisfaction, eager to share the secret of Truth. "Wish I could say I came upon it myself, but I didn't. A friend of mine back east discovered the property of the liquid less than a year ago. Harmless in itself, not toxic in the least. But when it comes into contact with lye soap residue, it turns a vivid, bloody, red."

In spite of himself, Tom grinned at the simplicity of it. "So it truly is random," he said. "When you said it wasn't so well-orchestrated . . ."

Teague took a mock bow. "I never claimed to have worked so hard."

"It's simply a matter of who has washed their hands with soap most recently."

"The more lye residue, the more *guilty* the suspect."

"I'll give you credit, Mr. Teague," Carpenter said, indicating the peddler's bulging pockets. "You seem to have stumbled into a lucrative market."

"Oh, this?" Teague patted his pockets and chuckled. "This is just change to whet the appetite. I can't make a living selling the bottled chemical water. I simply don't have enough supply."

"I don't think I understand."

Before Teague could reply, something

heavy hit the boardwalk in front of Tom's place. It was a shoe, and it came on the heels of another, even louder, spate of cursing and yelling.

Then came a groan of terror. And a cheer erupted from the mob.

Teague winked at Tom. "The front of my wagon is for carrying bottles of Truth. But that's only a small part of my actual freight. You see, I'm a wholesale seller, Mr. Carpenter. I sell to men like you, men with general merchandise stores."

Outside, somebody yelled "String him up."

Then: "Hang him!"

Inside, Tom turned from the doorway back to Teague. "Exactly what is it you sell?"

"Hang her, too!"

Teague smiled, revealing a row of perfect, white teeth. Expensive teeth.

"I sell rope, Mr. Carpenter. Miles and miles of fine, woven hemp rope." A chill ran down Tom Carpenter's spine.

Teague reached out to shake his hand. "I think we can make a wonderful business arrangement, sir. Don't you?"

GORDON'S KNOT

Stanley Gordon, OD, PhD, war hero decorated with the Silver Cross of the Emerald Knights of Valor, Methodist minister, and newly ordained mayor of Conversion Valley, Utah, had had it up to his beige bow tie with the whole damn town.

They could all go hang as far as he was concerned.

Especially the underhanded mercantile owner, John Peabody, and his two-dollar cans of runny peaches, three-bit thimble-size sips of sarsaparilla, and forty-to-a-box lead bullets going for a mere double gold eagle.

And of course, how could Stanley forget, the counterfeit postage stamps Peabody printed in his back room.

Conversion Valley's inflation rate was higher than a cat's back, but Stanley's blood pressure was outpacing it.

The last time Stanley had seen such

blatant price gouging was while he worked the high hill grade outside Salt Lake City and the tent saloon pickled the road crew's wallet on a nightly basis. At least the working men faced no imminent danger of liver damage from the tepid mugs of crick water and vinegar the place sold.

Right now, a similar scenario was going on at Jubal Warbly's Saloon here in Conversion Valley.

And on the subject of that particular den of evil — Stanley hadn't witnessed such prejudice against women and children since man-jacking a log slide in the Montana wilderness. Hadn't ministered to such a fatheaded lot of numbskulls since he cleared out the Devils Nest House of Virtuous Maids outside Laramie.

Add to that, everybody in town smelled like the carcass of a three-day dead mare in the middle of a hot July afternoon.

Conversion Valley had yet to convert to soap.

Naturally, petty crime was running as wild as everything — and everyone — else.

After giving it much reflection one Thursday's eve, the reverend carefully wrapped the limp remains of his supper, a bacon and egg sandwich on tough sourdough bread, in wax paper, put it on the steely cold surface of his cabin's cookstove for safekeeping, and donned his ebony coat and hat. Into his pocket he tucked a square of rich crème notepaper decorated with a heavy flow of black ink, a message for Anders Schmidt, the telegraph operator.

Across the back of the sheet, he'd printed out in a blocky hand: *To Tame a Town.*

Stanley's parsonage, little more than a one-room cabin, was affixed to the white-washed Methodist church, and Schmidt's telegraph was set up in the post office, a quarter mile straight down Main Street.

An autumn sunset streaked the Western panorama with swathes of orange and pink as Stanley took to the road. Fingers of indigo and brackish ebony whisps flowed out over the horizon to pile up in great towering bunches of dark, billowing thunderheads. His shoes kicked up the dust. The town could use a good soaking rain.

Baptize the whole lot of them, he thought. Better water than fire.

He stopped in the middle of the street to admire the oncoming storm. It was just the shot of drama his drooping spirits needed. Against a backdrop of unsanitary odors from the saloon's latrine and the scuffle of two dudes engaged in fisticuffs, the Lord's accomplished paintbrush buoyed Stanley

246

out of despair.

He studied the message he carried on the notepaper in hand.

To Tame a Town.

Perhaps if *tame* was too strong a verb, then *sanitize* was too clinical.

Tidy up, too domestic, and *dredge* perhaps a tad bit vulgar.

As Saddleback Sawyer, one of the town's newer arrivals and an unrepentant drunk, crashed through the front picture window of the Warbly Saloon, the first structure on the right, Stanley took in the wrecked shards of man and glass and decided tame was, in fact, just the right word indeed.

The next business up the line was Sara's hotel and café, and Stanley quickened his pace, hoping he could lope past the leaning three-story edifice without old Bent-Lung catching wind of his passage.

With the heavy soporific of fried liver and onions on the air, he didn't think Sara Bent-low would be paying much attention to anything outside her smoky kitchen.

He was wrong.

"And a good eve to ye, Mayor." Sara's voice was somewhere between the chuff of a steam engine and the dulcet tones of a tethered bobcat. Propped against one of her cracked front porch pillars beside her twenty-year-old daughter, she enunciated every word through a cloud of vapor, her omnipresent cigarette firmly fixed to her bottom lip. "Where is it you're off to with such a determined pace, Reverend?"

"Evening, Sara. It's the post office I'm headed for." The reverend mayor doffed his hat and addressed the girl. "How do, Miss Jenny?" Sara pulled herself away from the post and shoved her girl roughly aside.

"You wouldn't be mailing a late-night love note to some sweetie back east, now would ye? Not with so many of us widow gals pining for you here? It really wouldn't be fair to us."

Stanley swallowed the bitter taste in his mouth. His love life, or lack of one, was a constant running joke with Sara. But he gave as good as he got. "You know I'm saving my heart for you, Sara, dear."

Her cackle reverberated on the small bones of his ear. "It'll be a cold day in hell, won't it?"

"As you say, Sara. As you say."

She turned her attention back to her child. "What the devil are you still doing here? Didn't I tell you to get back inside?"

Stanley pushed up the street as fast as his forty-year-old legs would carry him.

He ducked into the post office as a fresh

wind raced past and lightning traced the contour of clouds.

"Seeking shelter from the storm, Rev?" Anders Schmidt had the bald red pate of a turkey vulture and hunched shoulders to match. Standing behind the walnut counter with an amused turn of the cheek, he pushed his spectacles up his long, hooked beak and waited.

"Storm is right," Stanley said. "And more than one kind of squall out there tonight." He laid his message out on the polished wood surface. "I'm praying for a change in the weather."

Schmidt read the first line. "To Tame a Town," he said. Then his eyes quickly ran back and forth over the fine penmanship.

Forefinger scratching his chin, Schmidt shook his head. "Nope. Nope, it'll never work."

"You read the message?"

"I did."

"You understand what it is?"

"It's an advertisement. You're looking for a lawman."

"Town marshal," Stanley recited from memory. "Weekly pay. Room provided. Position to be filled immediately."

Again, Schmidt wasn't supportive. "I don't like it."

Stanley contained the pressure building inside. He had expected some pushback to his plan. Now that Schmidt had seen the message, there was nothing to do but see everything through to its conclusion. "Conversion Valley's got the makings of a good town," Stanley said, "but with the kind of folks running Main Street, we're spiraling down the drain."

Schmidt turned up his peaked nose. "You exaggerate, sir. And to air our laundry to strangers? To solicit a hired gun?"

Stanley hooked a thumb over his shoulder. "The way I'm feeling tonight, if this were twenty years ago, I'd be down there at Warbly's with a gun of my own. Of course, that was before I heard the Lord's calling and took up the cloth."

"I'm on your side, Mayor." Schmidt added the honorific with a sly grin.

But Stanley knew a lie when he heard it. In fact, he counted on Anders Schmidt being against him.

A few drops of rain spattered against the windows, and lightning flashed on the western horizon.

Schmidt said, "Hear me out."

"Fair enough. Tell me why I shouldn't do everything in my power to bring law and order to Conversion Valley."

"Oh, I'm not against law and order. As I said, I'm against a hired gun."

Stanley shook his head. "It's not so much a gun I want. It's a lawman."

"Out here on the frontier? Same thing." Schmidt pointed at the slip of paper on the counter. "You go posting that in the *Salt Lake Tribune,* or send it to Denver and Santa Fe, you're gonna get a dozen ruffians applying for the job in person. Each and every one of them will have a collection of notches on their pistols and something to prove on their mind."

"I hope to the good Lord you're right," Stanley said as he gripped the door handle.

Schmidt continued. "You know how it is. You've been there. You've talked about it yourself when recounting your past. On the railroad, working in Montana. You've been around hard men. A month or two with a new marshal and you'll be advertising for a second mortician."

The conversation was interrupted as the outside door opened with a crash, and John Peabody poured into the room, a towering waterfall with a perpetual sneer.

Stanley greeted him. "Hello, John."

"I saw the lamp light on. Gotta drop a postcard into the mail."

Schmidt said, "Certainly, Mr. Peabody.

251

Come in, come in."

"I appreciate it, Anders." The merchant plodded into the room and propped his massive frame up on the counter. Once situated, he flipped a postcard down and dug into his trousers, presumably for change. When, apparently, he couldn't find any coins, he produced a bright red postage stamp instead.

From a pot on the counter, Schmidt applied a dollop of flour paste. "A letter to your aunt, is it?"

"Yes, 'tis." He poked his chin out at the missive. "She's ailing, you know."

"So I'd heard."

"I'll keep her in prayer," Stanley said.

"That makes one of us," Peabody said. "The old biddy just doesn't know when to give up the ghost." Anders pounded down the counterfeit stamp with his fist, then hand-cancelled the postage.

Stanley said, "Your aunt's been sick long?"

"My whole life." Peabody stood next to the mayor with liver and onions on his breath. "I tell you what, fellas, the world would be better off without her."

After the door closed behind him, the merchant's words left a chill in the room.

And his passage left a stink. Stanley said, "Peabody's been taking his suppers over at

Sara's café."

Schmidt sighed. "Those two are friendly as littermate kittens."

"Tell me something," Stanley said. "Would the world truly be better off without Peabody's aunt?"

"I don't know about the world, but Peabody would be better off."

Stanley said, "That's the impression I got."

"The old witch is rich as King Solomon, and Peabody is her only heir. You can see why he wants her out of the way."

"And him being one of our better citizens." Stanley nodded at the notice he had carried in. "Please send that advertisement as written. And charge it to the city."

When he opened the door, a fresh gust of rain blew in.

Stanley indicated Schmidt's dark, oiled slicker hanging on a hook. "Seeing as you live in the back, I don't suppose you'll be going out anymore tonight?"

"No, I won't."

"Do you mind if I borrow the slicker? Hate to catch pneumonia before Sunday worship."

Schmidt accepted the request with a wave. "Go right ahead."

Watching the rain turn the dusty street into muddy puddles, Stanley Gordon traipsed home with his hands and chin tucked firmly into Schmidt's coat. Pictures of the townsfolk needled him. Peabody's fleshy sneer. Schmidt, the old vulture. Sara slapping Miss Jenny.

Only a beginning.

"This town's in a hell of a knot," he said to himself. "It's a Gordian Knot is what it is."

Stanley picked up his sandwich from the cookstove and retired to bed. Oblivious of crumbs, he chewed the hard bread, gazing at the dripping slicker, working it all out for the tenth time in his head. Then he drifted off to sleep.

For better, or for worse, his plan was underway.

He knew Schmidt would never send the telegram advertising for a marshal.

He was counting on it.

And then the knot would start to unravel.

Early the next morning, Stanley Gordon sat at Sara Bentlow's dining room table, sipping cold, bitter coffee, writing on the back of a postcard. The room smelled of stale fried lard and caked-on grime, and spiders crawled around the ceiling corners.

The pen being mightier than the sword, Stanley thought optimistically as he finished striking his second blow against the rascals of Conversion Valley.

When he stood up to visit the privy, he called out to the kitchen. "I'll return shortly, Sara. Please save my spot at the table and keep an eye on my things to make sure no one disturbs them."

No response from Sara, but he knew she heard him.

Once outside, he snuck around back and discreetly peered back inside through a dirty window. As he suspected, Sara had emerged from the kitchen and took him at his word. Having picked up his postcard, she was busy reading its contents.

She stood with her crooked back arched to the side, a flat hand on one hip, the other holding the card up to her nearsighted eyes. While Stanley watched through the window, Sara's daughter came into the dining room carrying a tin coffeepot. "Shoo away, Jenny," Sara said. "Git back to the kitchen."

"But I thought —"

"I said, git!" Sara threatened her with a flailing fist.

Stanley figured there was a special location in the underworld for abusive people. If so, Sara reserved her spot each and every day.

When he saw Sara place the postcard back

down on the table, he went back inside.

He arrived at the table just as Sara emerged from the kitchen. "Fresh coffee?" she said.

"I must be living right," Stanley replied, returning to his chair. The postcard had been replaced to its original location on the table. He held up his tin cup.

Sara asked, "What are you writing there?"

"Postcard to a friend."

"Anyone I might know?"

Stanley pretended to think about it. Then, lowering his voice, he said, "Confidentially, Sara, I'll be making some changes soon."

"Oh?" A bad actor, she tried to feign surprise, but her glee at being brought in on the postcard's secret was authentic.

Stanley continued with his story. "I'm going to be coming into a great deal of money. Sooner rather than later."

"I see." The coffeepot all but trembled out of Sara's grip, and Stanley laid his hands on Sara's forearm, guiding her into the chair next to him.

"You might have heard about Mr. Peabody's aunt. Poor thing isn't long for this world."

"Yes . . . I had heard the news."

"It turns out Aunt Hilda is a distant relation of mine as well."

"Is she at that?"

Stanley delivered the punch line with a sober face. He couldn't help but think of all those Montana roughnecks he used to play poker with in the days before he was ordained.

The Lord did indeed work in mysterious ways

He'd learned to lie from the best.

"Aunt Hilda's changed her will to make me her sole heir." He crossed his lips with his index finger. "Don't breathe a word of this to Peabody."

Sara was transfixed.

Stanley had seen her read the postcard he wrote. In it, he thanked Hilda for the honor of his future inheritance. Now Sara was openly privy to the knowledge.

There was no reason not to believe everything Stanley told her was true.

Now came the coup de grâce. Stanley cleared his throat. "I hope I'm not being too forward, Sara. But I'd like you to share in my good fortune."

"You . . . you would?"

"We joke about it a lot, but . . . would you . . . I mean, could you see your way to . . ."

Sara couldn't hold it in. "Marry you?"

"Yes. Marry me?" Now Stanley moved his

finger to Sara's lips. "Don't answer right away. Let it sit a spell."

"But I don't have to let it sit. I want to say *yes!*"

"We'll elope, darling. This very weekend. You can leave the hotel to Jenny."

The immediacy of it was taking away her breath.

Stanley stood up. "Visit me at the parsonage later tonight. Let's say, around eight o'clock." He patted her hand., "Remember, don't breathe a word to a living soul."

By noon, everybody in Conversion Valley knew Stanley Gordon, OD, PhD, war hero decorated with the Silver Cross of the Emerald Knights of Valor, Methodist minister, and newly ordained mayor, was going to be married to Miss Sara Bentlow, widow of old Herman Bentlow and proprietor of the Bentlow Hotel and Café.

They knew Sara was leaving the hotel to her daughter, Jenny, because Stanley was coming into a fortune. They would elope before the weekend was over.

No one expected them to stay in Conversion Valley.

"But it's a damned lie," Peabody said, knocking an empty beer bottle to the barroom floor. "There's no way Hilda's leaving her money to him. Gimme another one, Jubal."

Gray-headed, with a lazy eye and a spider-shaped port wine stain on his cheek, Jubal Warbly stood behind the bar and supplied Peabody with a third dollop of whiskey. Then he handed a second drink to Anders Schmidt.

"Sara says they're leaving all right," Schmidt said.

"Which is fine with me," said Jubal. "This talk of the mayor out fishing for a lawman has got me spooked."

"Aw, you know I didn't send that message," Schmidt said.

"Just knowing Gordon is leaning in such a direction scares me," Jubal said. "There's pasteboards out there with my mug on 'em. Did you know that? And it ain't easy to hide a mug like mine. We get a badge-toter in this town, I'm gonna have to go."

"I told you, I didn't send the message."

"I feel like the mayor is deliberately trying to shake me."

"By next week, he'll be gone," Schmidt said.

Peabody slurred his words. "I tell ya, it's a lie."

"It's not a lie," Stanley said from the doorway. He held up his hand, "None for me, Jubal. Thanks."

Peabody closed one eye, guzzled half his bottle's contents, then scratched his prodigious triple chin. "You're making all of this up, Mr. Mayor."

"I'm not." Stanley strolled in and pulled a chair from beneath one of the round tables. He sat down as Peabody swallowed more beer.

"You have to admit it's hard to believe," Schmidt said.

Stanley slid a postcard across the table. "Since you all seem to have heard the news, I'm not shy about sharing my sources."

On the front of the postcard was a drawing of a duck. On the back was a short message written in a flowery hand.

Peabody snatched it up. He couldn't deny it looked for all the world like his aunt's handwriting, and it stated in clear, concise terms that Stanley Gordon was to be Hilda Peabody's only heir.

The mayor leaned back in his chair, lifting the front legs off the floor. He laced his fingers behind his head and sighed. "The Lord's work is a wonder to behold, don't you think?"

Peabody tossed the postcard back to the table. "You got some kind of gall, mister."

Stanley shook his head. "I should have

known Sara couldn't keep our love a secret." He opened his arms. "A love like ours is just too big to contain."

"Is it?"

"It is, indeed," Stanley said,

Schmidt said, "I don't remember delivering that postcard."

"No reason you should, is there? It's not like you're reading all the mail before you deliver it to people."

Schmidt wasn't so easily put off. "I . . . don't know."

Stanley said, "In case you didn't notice, I brought your slicker back." He pointed at the hall tree beside the saloon's batwing doors. "It's supposed to rain again this evening. I thought you might need to wear it."

Then Stanley clapped his hands and stood up from the table. "Now, I must be off. So much to do, so little time."

Peabody couldn't resist a parting shot. "Go to hell," he said.

"Already been there," Stanley said. "I'm aiming for better."

Back at the parsonage, his partner in crime waited in the foyer with bacon and egg sandwiches. "It's the last of the sourdough bread," she said. "Until I can bake some more."

Stanley thanked her and devoured a third of his late lunch.

"Has Mother spread the word all over town?"

Young Jenny Bentlow shined with the innocence of Job, and Stanley almost felt a pang of regret for drawing her into his scheme.

Almost.

He filled her in while she nibbled at her bread.

"Everybody knows the story," Stanley said. "Everybody is fairly skeptical."

"What about Peabody?"

At the crooked merchant's name, Stanley's resolve reasserted itself. "He won't hurt you again." Jenny rubbed her arms as if she were cold. "I feel so foolish, the way he led me on."

"You're not to blame, dear."

"When I think of how he touched me. How Mother encouraged him to . . . to . . ."

For the girl's sake, Stanley tamped down his temper. "You were right to come to me."

"I don't want anybody hurt," Jenny said.

"After all they've done, they've earned a hurting."

"But you said —"

Stanley offered her a grim smile. "Like I recently told somebody, I'm a man of the cloth now. I won't live by violence."

While Jenny composed herself, Stanley gathered together the numerous postcards strewn along his coffee table.

Postcards from Aunt Hilda Peabody, written to her nephew, John.

Postcards Jenny had craftily lifted from Peabody's boudoir and studied until she could mimic the old lady's handwriting.

Stanley tossed the counterfeit postcard from the saloon onto the pile.

"Does Peabody believe you're going to elope with my mother?"

"As I said, they are skeptical."

"Mother certainly isn't. She told me just this morning that you're what she's been waiting for ever since Dad died a dozen years ago."

"Has she signed over the hotel to you, yet?"

"She's planning to do it tonight right before she comes to see you."

"Good. The Gordian Knot is coming undone. One strand at a time."

"The what?"

"It's an old story."

"I don't know it."

Stanley did his best to explain. "In the days before Christ, Alexander marched through Gordium, the capital of Phrygia.

There, he confronted an ox-cart with its yoke lashed to a pole by means of a large, intricate knot."

"This is Alexander the Greek you're talking about?"

"Alexander the Great, yes." Stanley continued. "A local fortune-teller had decreed that whoever could loosen the knot would be the future ruler over all of Asia."

"No way Alex would miss such an opportunity."

"But rather than take time to untie the knot, he simply used his sword and cut the knot in two."

"Smart cookie," Jenny said.

Stanley corrected her. "Maybe not so smart. Some versions of the myth suggest that by cutting the knot instead of untying it, Alexander cheated, and was rewarded with death as soon as he fulfilled the prophesy of ruling over all creation."

Jenny chewed on the lesson and seemed to understand without any more words.

The people of Conversion Valley are a tangled bunch, but Stanley didn't intend to cut through them with a sword — or gun.

"Better to untie the knot one strand at a time," he said. "You'll make sure Peabody and Schmidt are at the mercantile by nine?"

Jenny nodded. "They'll be there."

■ ■ ■ ■

At eight o'clock, Sara Bentlow arrived at the church dressed in a long linen gown, threadbare to be sure, but Stanley assumed it was the best of the Bentlow wardrobe. She had rouge on her cheeks and a ribbon tied to a lock of her hair. She reminded Stanley of a fishing lure he'd once borrowed from his brother.

Stanley sunk into her arms with mock despair.

And artificially induced tears.

Numbed by her daily culinary chores, Sara couldn't smell the sliced onions in the kitchen.

"What's the matter with ye, dearie?" she said. "Come tell Sara all about it?"

"I have no words," Stanley said. He wagged his head like he'd lost his dog in a raffle. "I'm beyond heartbroken."

"I can't help if I don't know what's the matter, love." Together they recessed to the foyer of the little place and reclined on a daybed.

"Fortunes come. And fortunes go," Stanley said.

"Fortunes . . . go?" Sara's painted cheeks fell like August crab apples.

"She's changed her mind again, Sara. Aunt Hilda has opted to leave her money to Peabody after all."

Sara recoiled as if stung by a hornet. "You're not serious?"

"Serious as a mud hen under the hatchet."

"When did you find out?"

"Only this evening. A fresh note came in the mail." Stanley handed her one of Jenny's bogus cards, but Sara didn't bother reading it.

Instead, she slumped against the back of the couch. "We were so close to having our dreams . . ."

Stanley showed her his open palms. "I'm still yours if you'll have me."

Sara's eyes shuttled left to right, taking in the cramped quarters. Without Hilda's payout, the nuptials weren't as inviting.

Before she could reply, Stanley snapped his fingers. "There's still a way!"

Sara shot off the couch like she'd been launched from a cannon. "Is there? Tell me, dearest."

"If we can't take it from one Peabody, we'll take it from the other."

"I don't understand."

"You've been in the back of the mercantile building. More, I know you've got John Peabody's ear. How much would you say a stack of his counterfeit postage stamps was worth?"

Sara understood the question, but all Stanley suggested was slow to dawn on her. "I don't know what they would be worth. Quite a lot, I suppose."

"Quite a lot indeed. What if you were to . . . shall we say, borrow several sheets? Say, a reasonably small stack?" He held his finger and thumb an inch apart. "We could take the sheets out of the county with us."

"And sell them." Sara caught wind of Stanley's enthusiasm. "Darn right we could sell them!"

Running with it, her arms and legs were animated. Too excited to sit, she leapt to her feet and paced. "I wonder how much we could get per sheet? I know he's sold a bundle of them to Schmidt for at least five dollars per sheet, and there must be . . ."

"I'd guess a thousand sheets," Stanley said.

"More than that," Sara said.

"He won't miss a few hundred sheets, will he?"

"No," Sara grinned. "He won't. And it's not like he's going to call in the law and ask them to track down a bunch of counterfeit stamps."

"You've been in his print room, haven't

you? Do you know where the sheets are?"

"Oh, yes," Sara said. "Pea-brain shows off the entire operation any chance he gets."

"I knew you were friends . . ."

"Not so much anymore."

"I'll drive you over to the mercantile in my wagon."

They rode together on Stanley's buckboard wagon, pulled by his gray mare. Beside the wide mercantile building, in a parking space of thin grass and weeds, he set the brake, careful not to wake Saddleback Sawyer as he slept off his latest episode of drunkenness.

The reflection of a full harvest moon floated in the dark store windows, an enormous round orange.

Stanley followed Sara around the imposing frame structure and through a back door.

"We won't light a lantern," Sara said. "I know where the stamps are."

The cluttered room was stuffy and ran the entire length of the public front. Separated from the retail space by a series of tall studs and a tin wall, its perimeter was lined with stuffed shelving and full cabinetry. Sara threaded her way through tins of paint and printers' ink, then straight to an open rack near a tall steel printing press. "Here they are!"

As Sara announced her success, a kerosene lamp lit the scene.

"Who goes there?"

"What's going on?"

"Mother?"

Stanley edged toward the door he and Sara had used to enter the cluttered room. Lamp held high in hand and flanked by Jenny and Schmidt, Peabody confronted Sara. "I'll ask again, what's going on?"

At the back door, Stanley whistled, and Saddleback Sawyer melted out of the shadows. The lanky young man now seemed completely sober and in full control of his senses. He took one final drag off his cigarette, then dropped it to the ground and crushed it underfoot. "This is the operation you told me about?"

"Yes, it is."

Then Jenny was beside them.

Across the room, Sara was defiant with a stack of counterfeit red stamps in hands. She flung an outstretched arm toward the door where Stanley waited.

"It's all his doing," she said.

"I'll straighten this out," said Sawyer, walking into the light, his U.S. Marshal's badge gleaming.

"Schmidt's in on it too, Marshal," Stanley said.

"I have no idea what you're talking about," Schmidt said. "And what's this about a marshal?"

"Turns out I made a mistake the other night," Stanley said. "Here I thought I needed to advertise, but wouldn't you know we already had a marshal in town."

"Right under your nose," Sawyer said. "Like the Good Book says, the Lord will provide."

"Saddleback Sawyer?" Schmidt said. "But you're a drunk! You've been a drunk ever since you wandered into town."

Sawyer grinned. "That's sort of what I wanted you to think."

"It doesn't matter. I still say I know nothing about these stamps."

Stanley cleared his throat. "I'm glad you're wearing your coat, Schmidt. Check the side pocket, and you'll find the evidence there."

Schmidt patted his pocket. "I don't understand. What do you —" He reached in and pulled out a folded sheet of stamps. A sheet of stamps identical to the ones Sara held in her hand.

Stanley said. "Imagine that."

Schmidt's bald pate went purple with

rage. "Stanley Gordon, you set this up."

Peabody and Sara started yelling then, too.

Sawyer let out a pent-up breath and pulled his six-shooter from a holster under his coat.

The room was immediately silent.

"We'd like to unravel all this without violence," Stanley said. "But if you all force the marshal's hand, well then that's a solution too."

Schmidt quickly waved his hands. "No, no violence."

Sara said, "I'm a peaceful woman. Stanley knows that. Don't you, dearest?"

He turned to lead Jenny outside with the petition still ringing in his ears. "Dear heart? Darling?"

"Cold day in hell, Sara," he said. Then to Jenny, "I hope I wasn't too hard on her."

"No harder than she was on me. On more than one person over the years."

Stanley bit his bottom lip. "In the end, it still took a gun to calm them down."

"Didn't you tell me that the Gordian Knot was actually a series of smaller knots wound together?"

"Yes."

"There's still a lot of work here to be done. A lot to untangle." She took his arm gently and led him off to the wagon. "So far, you've shown a sword, but you haven't had to use it."

"I suppose you're right, Miss Jenny. I suppose it's a good start."

She agreed. "Yes, it's a start."

Sister to a Buzzard

The tremendous graveyard explosion rousted Wilkes City, Kansas, just after midnight with rattling windows and a thundering echo loud enough to wake the dead.

Or at least blast them to bits.

My uncle Ron Stark was the elected sheriff, and it was his friend the mayor, Bill Strickland, who first called Rufus McAllister "the brother to a buzzard." But it wasn't old Rufus who was going around robbing graves in the summer of 1890.

"It might be me who finally stops 'em," Rufus said when he joined me in the middle of the moonlit street, pulling a jacket on against the October chill. "Let's go find out, girl."

"Let me get my shoes on, and I'll catch up."

When Rufus picked me to help catch the resurrection men, Uncle Ron had pitched eleven kinds of a fit.

Meeting me on the front porch of our house as I tugged on my cowboy boots, he wasn't any happier. One look at the smoky haze floating over the cemetery, and he knew what happened.

"This is that old buzzard's doing, isn't it?"

"Rufus doesn't deserve all the names you call him. Dirty Codger. Brother to a Buzzard. He's helping you track these grave robbers from the goodness of his heart. He doesn't have to help you."

I got one boot half-on, stood up, and stamped it home. Uncle Ron shook his head.

"Goodness of his heart. Along with me forgiving a year's worth of drunk and disorderly charges against him."

"Along with your forgiveness, yes. But that ain't the most of it."

Uncle Ron watched as the citizens of Wilkes City wandered out of their houses to see about the commotion. He brushed at his bushy red mustache and shook his head. "I don't like you friending him, Pepper. The man's an admitted criminal with no real ties to our town." He put his hand on my shoulder. "You're my only niece, and your ma and pa trusted me with your upkeep before they passed on. I've got a responsibility — a duty to uphold my promise to them."

"I've never given you any reason to distrust me, have I?"

I couldn't help but throw that one in.

Trust me, good behavior always pays off in the end. If in no other way than invoking it every now and again just to vex your elders.

Uncle Ron couldn't deny me. "You just be careful out there," he said. "These cemetery prowlers are the lowest kind of human being. They're akin to rats and mice, and I don't have to remind you that Rufus McAllister was once numbered in their kith."

"Fine and good, but don't forget — you have a responsibility to the county, too, Sheriff," I said. "A duty to uphold the law. With these resurrection men digging up the graves of prominent families, you aren't gonna get a chance to sleep until you bring them in."

"Ain't nobody gonna sleep if Rufus sets another damned booby trap."

We hurried off together to the graveyard.

Rufus McAllister was barely five feet tall with stooped shoulders, and I guessed if he stood straight he'd add another seven or eight inches. His hair hung long to his shoulders like General Custer but instead of yellow and smooth it was all snarled up like a kitten had been through it. His beard was slightly better tended and hugged his face like a gray scarf.

In a red checked shirt with clean pants and coat, he dressed better than he once did. Smelled better too.

Inside the cemetery gates, all we could smell was powder smoke and wet dirt while Rufus did a jig around a crater the size of Florida.

"Lookee, here," he said, holding up a ragged coffin lid. "Blew the lid clean off old Marley Collins."

"Dammit, man," Uncle Ron said as we closed in on the wrecked gravesite. "I didn't authorize anything like this."

I kicked at a hunk of burnt rock and a cold breeze drew the dust into ghostly swirls. The carnage was more than a little bit overwhelming.

Hunks of the Collins casket, along with Collins himself, were scattered over half an acre, and one section of the yard's wrought iron fence was twisted and bent. Clods of dirt and clay were everywhere, and it was hard to walk a straight line through the debris.

Having worked with munitions during the war between the states, Rufus had used a contraption he called a "coffin torpedo" that was triggered by a pressure plate inside the casket. His hope was to first disable the grave robbers when they opened the top, but more: "Plant the fear deep inside their hearts."

Rufus crowed. "What do you think, Pep?"

"I think it might be hard to identify the villain's remains."

"Yeah, I might've got carried away."

Ron faced Rufus over the smoking pit. "I don't approve of this at all."

"You ain't got a lot of choices left, Sheriff."

Which was more than a little bit true.

Mrs. Matilda Matthias had only the day before promised to drive Uncle Ron from office if he didn't stop the resurrection men. Old man Matthias was on her mind — her dear, departed brother, recently deprived of his gold wedding ring, cuff links, and tie tack in the afterlife.

While Uncle Ron and Rufus argued, I glanced into the grave and saw what remained of the remains of Marley Collins, his top half still slumbering away under the silver moon, both hands clasped across his chest in eternal prayer. I swallowed hard and looked away.

Rufus straightened a tipping headstone, then picked up another chunk of wood. Whistling.

Uncle Ron rubbed his forehead. "This won't do."

I said, "Rufus turned over a new leaf when he found the Lord. All he wants to do is help."

Ron opened his mouth with a counter-argument poised on his tongue.

But further conversation was interrupted by the arrival of Mayor Bill and news from the streets of town.

"The rotten bastards struck again," he said. "Howdy, Pepper." Mayor Bill always tipped his hat and treated me like a lady. I hate to say I always blushed, but I always did.

"I think Rufus got 'em this time," I said.

Mayor Bill took in the destruction but shook his head. "Maybe got one of 'em. But they were out in force tonight." He continued on. "They also struck outside the Norwood place. There's a little family plot over there with less than a dozen stones. Naturally, they went for the patriarch. Dug him up and took a passel of silver."

The sheriff said, "No doubt he had the most prominent header?"

"And most recently passed."

"Dirt's easier to move that'a way," Rufus said, joining us. "Nobody wants to work harder than they have to."

"We're gonna get some complaints about this," said the sheriff, gesturing toward the exploded gravesite. Looking past the mayor, I saw a dozen people gathering around the cemetery gates, craning their necks, whispering.

"Especially with nothing to show for it," Uncle Ron said.

"I wouldn't say that," Rufus said. "At least now we've got a lead on this devil's identity."

"Oh? Who is he?"

Rufus held up a bloody stump of an arm. "Whoever this belongs to." He nodded down toward Marley Collins in the grave. "I don't think old Marley had three arms. Besides, this one's still warm."

Six hours later, the first rays of morning sun lit the sheriff's office, and I sat on the opposite side of Uncle Ron's desk next to Mayor Bill.

"Morning, all." Rufus walked in the open door, and Ron stood up and crossed the room to his two-drawer filing cabinet. Hitting him right at his gunbelt, the top of the cabinet doubled as a place to set the tin coffeepot he carried over from the café every morning.

"Coffee's good and hot, who wants some?"

He dropped a dollop into his own tin cup and took a drink.

Mayor Bill raised his hand, extending his coffee cup. "Thanks, Sheriff."

"Coffee, Rufus?" Ron lifted his tin pot.

Rufus shook his head and pulled a wood folding chair away from the office wall, then he sat down beside me before addressing the mayor. "Tell us more about the Norwood cemetery job."

"Can't a man even drink his coffee first?"

Rufus was all business. "I ain't here to socialize."

Uncle Ron sat back down behind his desk, and Bill held up his hands feigning helplessness. He said, "There's nothing more to tell than what I said last night. Sometime after ten o'clock — and before your explosion in town — Silas Norwood's grave was defiled."

I wondered out loud how they knew it was after ten o'clock.

Bill answered, "The widow Norwood was sitting up on her porch until then. She's got a clear view of the family plot, and you'll remember, we had a full moon."

Rufus said, "What all got stolen?"

"Silver cutlery, place setting, and a coffee urn."

"I wish folks would stop burying their valuables," said Uncle Ron. "It's just plain stupid, and it ain't like any dead fella's going to need 'em. And it's nothing but a temptation."

"Fifty dollars in gold double eagles, too," the mayor said.

The sheriff nodded. "Foolishness."

Rufus said, "How'd they get inside the box?"

Bill raised an eyebrow. "Pardon me?"

"The box, the coffin. How'd they get inside? Did they pry it open at the clasp or chop a hole in it with an ax? Did they dig around the entire thing and haul it out of the ground, or did they just tear up the lid?"

"I don't know what difference it makes."

"Makes all the difference," Rufus said. "Different men have different methods. Some men are patient. Methodical. Other men are in a hurry. It makes them sloppy."

"These men seemed methodical enough. They uncovered most of the casket, pried open the lids. No different than the last few jobs."

"And you say they got away with some kitchenware and some coins."

"Silverware. A coffee urn," Bill said.

"And double eagles," I said.

Rufus said, "What about the purse?"

"What purse?"

"The purse. The satchel. The container the gold coins were in. Or did the Norwoods just sprinkle them around the corpse like mint leaves?"

Mayor Bill didn't like Rufus, but I don't think I ever saw him so annoyed. He'd been asked a question he couldn't answer, and he didn't like it.

"We didn't find any kind of purse. I can't see what difference it would make if we did."

"My experience with these things, nine times out of ten, the family leaves money in the grave, they'll put it in a purse or satchel. If you don't find the satchel, it means the resurrection men carried away the loot. Probably on a horse or wagon." Rufus chuckled. "On the rare occasion you do find the purse, it'll be empty and near the opened tomb."

He looked straight at me and said, "Then what would you think, Pepper?"

"Maybe the robber stuffed the coins in his pockets," I said. "Maybe he didn't have so far to travel."

"That's been my experience," Rufus said.

Mayor Bill sighed. "That's the dumbest thing I've heard all day."

Rufus just grinned like the cat who swallowed the cream.

The sheriff said, "What about your third arm, Rufus? Any more ghoulish discoveries which might shed some light on all this?"

"Not so's I could find, no."

"It's simple," I said. "All we need to do is find a man with one arm."

"Unless he's already dead," Rufus said.

"May he rest in pieces."

Ron frowned at me. "That's enough, Pepper."

"The girl's got a point," Rufus said. "We find a man with one arm."

"Or a silver coffee urn," I said.

Rufus agreed. "Either way."

After we left the sheriff's office, I said, "Bill doesn't like you too much, does he?"

Rufus snuffed all the way down his throat into his lungs and wiped his nose on the sleeve of his coat. "I don't suppose I've ever given him reason to like me."

"You're a good man. You're helping stop these criminals. He should recognize it."

"The world doesn't always work according to our shoulds."

"Maybe if we find these grave robbers it'll help your reputation."

"I'd like to think so."

"What do we do first?"

"I'd like to visit the Norwood cemetery. See if I notice anything Bill missed."

"It's three miles north of town," I said. "I'll saddle up my horse."

"Better yet, we'll take my wagon."

But as we walked across the street we were stopped before we could get there. Two men blocked our path; both were dressed in black with pearl-handled revolvers on their hips. They looked just alike. Like brothers. Like killers.

Cain and Abel.

The taller one of the two said, "Got a message for you, Rufus McAllister."

"Get behind me, Pepper."

"Rufus — ?"

"Now," he said. Firm, without raising his voice. I got behind him.

"Don't worry. We aren't gonna kill you, old man. Not yet."

The second man spoke then, and his voice was slick and dark like calf scours.

"Stay away from the sheriff's office. There's nothing there that's any of your business."

"Sheriff Ron is my uncle," I said, poking my head out from behind Rufus's coat.

"You go make some friends your own age, missy. Older gentlemen like Rufus often pass away real sudden-like."

"Yeah," the first man said. "Real sudden-like."

Then they spun on their heels like soldiers and marched away toward the saloon.

"Do you know who those men were, Pepper?" Rufus said.

"No," I said, steeling myself for the worst answer possible. "Who were they?"

"I don't know. That's why I was asking you."

I jumped out into the street. "Darn it, I thought you'd say it was the Gorman Brothers or the Doering Gang, or the Bedlows from Tennessee."

"Nope, never saw 'em before in my life. But one thing's for certain. Our little black powder package did just what I hoped."

"Did it?"

"It put the fear in them."

I didn't want to argue with him, but Cain and Abel didn't seem overly frightened. On the other hand, they had sure put the fear into me.

"Are we still going over to the cemetery? Even after what they said?"

"Now, more than ever. You heard the man. I might pass on at any time, and I hope to get this all wrapped up before then."

But our trip was nearly fruitless.

Nearly — because in the end, we found

the coin purse Rufus predicted would be there.

Which, according to Rufus, meant the thief was local.

But after the better part of the afternoon snooping around the Norwood land, and finding nothing else of value, Rufus called it quits and drove me home past the mayor's house. He dropped me off at the sheriff's office.

"I'll be seeing you, Pep."

"Be seeing you, Rufus."

I climbed down from the wagon, but before he snapped the reins over his mules, he said, "I'm sorry if I got you in Dutch with your uncle. Maybe that owlhoot with the gun today was right."

"I don't understand."

"That joke you made about resting in pieces. Some folks wouldn't think it too funny. You'd do better finding a better caliber person than me to spend time with."

It wasn't so much what he said, but how he said it put a lump in my throat.

"Talk to you tomorrow?" I said.

"Tomorrow."

Damn Cain and Abel for putting a wedge between me and Rufus.

Between me and Uncle Ron.

If only there were a way to pin all this

grave-robbing business on the two of them.

I was so busy chewing over my problems, I didn't see the hotel marm, crazy Mrs. Sullivan and her pie plate eyes, until I almost ran into her on the boardwalk. She adopted a quick sideways gait as I stepped backwards at the last second. We narrowly missed a collision.

"I'm so sorry —"

"You watch your step, girl."

"Of course, ma'am, I —"

"You young people need to learn there's others in the world besides you. I've had it with the lot of you."

From her tone of voice and haggard look, I knew she was speaking to more than just a close call on the walk with me, but I didn't want to pry. Or, maybe I should say, I knew better than to pry, even if wanted.

Fortunately, I didn't have to ask any questions. Once Mrs. Sullivan started talking, it was like pulling a plug from a cider barrel. Her wild blue eyes practically spun around in circles.

"It's the same thing everywhere I go. And in my own hotel. You're no better than those young ruffians with the pearl-handled pistols rushing up and down my stairs at all hours of the night. Crashing about. Bang, bang. Pow! And don't think I didn't hear about your friend and that awful powder blast in the cemetery."

"We're trying to solve a series of crimes."

"At the expense of my guests. For the first time in forever, I have nearly a full house. Understand? Nary a vacancy. I can't afford for my guests to be woke up in the middle of the night. They're blaming me for the noise."

"What about these ruffians?" Her mentioning the pearl handles had my heart pounding. The more I found out about Cain and Abel, the more I'd find out about the grave robbers. "There's two of them, you say?"

"There's three of 'em, and not much older than you. I'm surprised you haven't already met them." She leaned in toward me, making a face. "How old are you, anyway?"

"I'm fifteen," I said.

"Just so."

She patted her hair into place and straightened her dress, and I was afraid I was going to lose her as she turned back to the boards, so I said, "Did these men give you a name? Why they're in town?"

Mrs. Sullivan wagged a finger at me. "I knew you'd poke your nose into it if given half the chance. I just knew it."

"I can't help but be curious."

"If you must know, they're here on business. And the only name they gave was Smith. John and Jack and Robert. One of them left on the stage this morning — Jack, I think. He took ill overnight, apparently."

"I'll just bet he did."

"Left without his guns."

"You might say he was no longer armed?"

She pinned me down with her crazy orbs. "What do you know about it?"

"Nothing," I said, remembering what Rufus said about my gallows humor. "But what business did you say these brothers were in?"

"I didn't say they were brothers, and I didn't say their business."

"Of course you didn't. I apologize."

"They're in the mortuary business."

A fact I related to Rufus the next day when I met him at the mercantile store.

"At least those boys are honest," he said. "From the looks of those gunbelts, I'd wager they put more people in the ground than most." Rufus picked up a silver sugar dish from the store counter and turned it over in his hands. "Did you tell your uncle what Mrs. Sullivan said?"

"Nope. Wanted to wait and tell you first."

"It'd be good if the sheriff asked them some questions. It's just a hunch, but I think they're working for somebody else."

"Is this like your guess about the purse? Based on experience?"

"Based on experience, yes."

"You and I could go ask them."

"Oh, no. I got the message loud and clear what they thought about me." Rufus shook his head. "Besides, we've got other work to do."

"What work?"

"You ain't heard the news? The widow Sophie Norwood passed away last night. Guess her heart just couldn't take the death of her brother."

"I'm sorry to hear it."

"I'm not. Don't you see, Pepper? This is the opportunity we need. Just like the blacksmith, we'll strike while things are red hot." He held up the silver sugar bowl. "And right here's the bait."

We waited a day, then at sundown we rode past the mayor's house and followed the winding road to the Norwood family plot. Once there, we found a tall mound of fresh dirt with a bouquet of wildflowers staked into the sod at its base.

Sophie didn't have a stone yet, but her place in her underground lodging was secure.

While Rufus lifted a shovel from the back of his wagon, he left me on the bench holding the silver sugar bowl with its four petite legs and tight-fitting lid. "I won't be a minute," he said, driving the head of the spade into the loose fill dirt. "Once we plant the bait, we'll set up the trap."

And some trap it was.

The Gardner machine gun was invented by a man named William Gardner in Toledo, Ohio, less than two decades before. That night, Rufus and I rigged one to sit on its tripod behind Silas Norwood's big stone and cover his sister's resting space. With its vertical magazine of .45 cartridges ready to pour forth from its muzzle as soon as anybody lifted the lid of Sophie's coffin, we were sure to bring the varmints down this time.

"It's a bit cold blooded, isn't it?" I said, riding back to town. "Spreading the word about the silver dish. Luring Cain and Abel out there to face an automatic firing squad."

"Let me tell you a story," Rufus said. "I wasn't much older than you when I took to the robbing of graves." He shrugged his shoulders, and his two mules carried us along the road back into Wilkes City. "The way I figured it, the dead got no use for all the gold and silver that gets buried with them. Shoveling loose soil is easy, and I didn't think I was hurting anybody. But one day that all changed."

"What happened?"

"A young woman lost her husband in a riding accident. They had only been married a short time, but they'd put all of the girl's dowry into a pair of matching gold rings for the two of them. The late groom was buried with that ring, and when I got wind of it, I stole it."

"It must've been worth quite a bit of money."

"It was, and after I cashed out, I was quite pleased with myself. For a while."

"Why only a while?"

"When the widow found out her husband's resting place had been disturbed, she got awfully upset. When she learned the ring was gone, it was more than she could bear. To her, marriage was an eternal bonding of the spirit. That ring symbolized the endurance of her everlasting commitment. Once it was gone, she felt she had truly lost everything."

I tried to imagine the grief the woman must've felt. "It sounds horrible."

"It was horrible, Pepper. And I was to blame." Rufus was quiet then, and the mules' hooves clip-clopped on the hard-packed road. Just when I thought the story was over, he said, "The widow threw herself off a bridge a week later."

"Oh, no."

"Now do you understand? I've never forgiven myself for that. By stealing that ring I killed her just as sure as if I'd pushed her off that bridge myself. Some people think it might be cold blooded, but these ghouls must be stopped. Like I should've been stopped."

I wasn't sure I understood. Not completely.

I wasn't sure I agreed with him.

But shortly before dawn, a volley of gunfire rose up in the direction of Norwood, the rapid-fire shattering of the peace I imagined the Gardner machine gun might make.

Rufus was there with the mayor when Uncle Ron and I arrived at the scene of the crime.

For the second time in less than twenty-four hours, the soil over Sophie's coffin had been cleared out. But this time, when the lid was removed, the trip wire had sprung, and the Gardner had flung thirty rounds of lead through the air. One of the Smith brothers caught most of the shots and looked like a weeping red pincushion sprawled out on the ground, his face a mask of surprise, his pearl-handled revolver still firmly stuck in its holster.

"We got one of them, anyway," Rufus said, before the mayor took charge.

"Which means his brother is free as a bird," Bill said. "I checked, and darned if they didn't get away with the silver sugar dish everybody was talking about at the café last night."

I shared a knowing look with Rufus.

Everybody was talking about the silver sugar dish, because she and Rufus had spread the word after planting it as bait. Obviously, somebody had tipped off the Smith brothers at the hotel.

But who?

Mrs. Sullivan? She certainly did her part to keep the gossip chain alive in Wilkes City.

And it was a fact the hotel had recently been tardy on paying its bills.

As the niece of the town sheriff, Pepper heard things.

"I'll bet this remaining Smith brother is holed up back at the hotel," I said. "Mrs. Sullivan told me they were staying there."

"It's the first place we'll look," Bill said. "Of course, he would know that."

"We'll start there anyway." Uncle Ron turned to Rufus and me. "This is the end, do you understand? Your traps may have brought results, but they're reckless. God forbid some innocent had stumbled out here into the path of that gun."

Rufus took the scolding with a grain of salt, but I decided Ron was right.

Seeing Mr. Smith chopped to ribbons wasn't pleasant. He asked for it . . . but did he *deserve* it?

We rode as far as Mayor Bill's house where he pulled into the drive. He called out, "Can I interest you in a cup of coffee before you hit town?"

"No, thank you, sir, we best be on about our grim business."

Rufus and I rode along on his wagon in silence while Uncle Ron pulled ahead on his gelding.

My mind kept wandering back to the ugly, sad picture of the slain resurrection man.

And then my stomach crawled up into my throat.

"Rufus?" I asked, hesitant, not sure I wanted to know the answer.

"Yesterday, when we set up the machine gun?"

"Yeah, Pepper?"

"You put the silver sugar dish inside the coffin, didn't you?"

"I did."

"And now it's gone."

"It is. That last Smith brother took it."

"Took it back to . . . where?"

"Back to whoever he's working for."

"What if he's working for Mrs. Sullivan?"

"If so, the sugar dish is at the hotel."

In my heart I knew the answer, but I had to ask the question. I could barely force out my next words. "You didn't . . . uh . . . rig the sugar dish?"

Rufus sighed. "I'm afraid so."

"With gunpowder? Wired to the lid?"

He looked at me, the weight of my words finally dawning on him. "All those people in the hotel . . ."

What had Mrs. Sullivan said?

For the first time in forever, I have nearly a full house. Understand? Nary a vacancy.

Rufus snapped the reins over and over.

Cracking like lightning he pushed the mules into a run. If there was any chance that sugar dish was in the hotel . . .

My heart chugged like a steam engine riding back to town, as did my friend's — judging from the worried expression on his face.

It was the longest three miles of my life. Fortunately, a search of the hotel revealed that the dish wasn't there. But if not there, where could it be?

Would another explosion wake us up in

the night?

Right there, I promised God and Jesus and the universe and anybody else who was listening that I would never, ever again play sister to a buzzard.

Never, ever again.

Mayor Bill Strickland tossed his hat onto the long fainting couch in his parlor. He hadn't been sleeping well the past few nights, what with all this Rufus McAllister business and the Smith brothers making such a bloody mess of everything.

He briefly considered taking a quick nap before following the sheriff into town, but naps made him sluggish, and he wanted to be on top of his game if Ron managed to capture the last Smith making his getaway. Bill wanted to be there in case of any questions.

Better coffee than a nap.

He walked casually to the warm cookstove, kindled a fire, and put a pot of water on to boil. Then he moved to the polished cedar sideboard with its iron coffee grinder and bone china cups.

A confirmed bachelor, Bill lived by himself and was glad for it. He had particular wants, and he wasn't afraid to admit he was persnickety and a bit selfish about his possessions. Some of his latest acquisitions were fine indeed.

As the water began to bubble behind him, he admired the fine, sterling silver coffee urn waiting for him to fill. He picked up the delicate silver spoon, so recently handed over to him by the Smiths.

Then, picking up a cup, he reached for his newest prize, a beautiful silver sugar bowl.

He lifted the lid.

A Gentleman Detective

Frank relaxed into the soft embrace of his chair, crossed his ankles, and kicked his shoes to the plush red Persian rug. While March filled the St. Louis streets with a heavy spring snow, amber gaslight added a warm ambience to Sue Ann Meeks's boardinghouse. The murmur of conversation from the other four guests lulled Frank into a comfortable doze.

Occasional sharp cheeps drifting down from the yellow finch Sue Ann kept in a large cage in the stairwell above added to his contentment.

Miss Thompson sat on Frank's right, a length of blue trailing up from the wicker basket full of yarn at her feet to a pair of clicking needles. As she spoke, she casually added another few inches to the striped blue scarf she had begun two nights before. "In all your natural born days, have you seen such a wintry bluster, Mr. Bail?"

Bail, who sat beside her in an oak rocker with an upholstered leather seat cushion, agreed that he had not. "But then again, I'm a Southern man, born and bred."

"Oh, my yes," the blonde said, "I keep forgetting. South Carolina, wasn't it?"

"Charleston, as a matter of fact."

Frank adjusted his shoulders, and Miss Thompson turned her head to address him. "Frank? Did you know Mr. Bail was from Dixie?" She told Bail, "Frank's a fellow Johnny Reb. I should say, he *was*. Back during the war."

Bail said, "A pleasure to know you, Frank."

Without opening his eyes, Frank nodded.

Miss Thompson chattered on, while Sue Ann served coffee to old Mrs. Cotton on the opposite side of the room.

"Sugar, dear?"

The old lady said, "Thank you," and her cat meowed. Frank peered through half-open lids as the striped tabby in her lap yawned.

"Mr. Brubeck?"

The old fellow next to Mrs. Cotton said, "None for me, Sue. It'll keep me awake for sure."

Miss Thompson continued to gush over Mr. Bail. "And aren't your bird carvings exquisite?"

Frank smiled to himself. Upon sitting down, he had admired the small, pine rendering under Bail's whittling blade.

Bail took Miss Thompson's compliment in stride. "Thank you, my dear."

"What else do you carve besides birds?"

"I have a series of life-sized ducks, a few miniature rabbits, occasionally I might carve a fish."

"Oh, you're a fisherman, too?"

Bail said he was. When Miss Thompson clicked her knitting needles together with delight, Frank decided it was the lady who was fishing.

"Coffee, Frank?"

He opened his eyes to redheaded Sue Ann with her silver urn and porcelain china cups. "I'll take a cup before bed," he said. "But only one. I do believe it's getting late."

Miss Thompson chimed in, "I so love a nice warm featherbed on a cold night. Don't you, Mr. Bail?"

Frank winked at Sue Ann as she handed him a warm cup. "Thank goodness for the Laclede gas fireplace," he said.

Three hours later, at precisely ten minutes after midnight, Frank sat in bed smoking his pipe, wide awake and regretting his after-supper catnap.

But it wasn't really the nap keeping him awake.

It wasn't even Mr. Brubeck's snoring. Tonight, the old man was sleeping soundly, as not even a muffled buzz came through the thin walls from the room next door where the old man was sleeping.

Frank wasn't as old as Brubeck, and so far as he knew he didn't snore.

What always kept him awake was the curse of a good memory and a hard life.

He'd seen ten times the horror of most folks. Quantrill made sure of that.

Suddenly, an excited series of exclamations came from the hallway outside his room. Sliding out from under the covers, Frank slipped the pipe into his pocket and tightened the belt of his sleeping gown as he walked toward his door.

Once in the hallway, he caught sight of Mr. Bail and Miss Thompson scurrying past a hall window in snow-reflected moonlight. Both descended the staircase in their bedtime attire — loose-fitting pajamas and housecoats. Both were calling to Sue Ann Meeks.

"It's the gas," shouted Bail. "By God, it's the gas."

"Get out, Miss Meeks. Everybody needs to get out."

At the foot of the stairs, Sue Ann opened her bedroom door. "What's this about the gas?"

Frank stood at the top of the stairs where the finch's wire birdcage hung suspended over the bannister from a hook in the ceiling. He didn't hear any chirping.

"The bird's dead, Sue Ann," Bail said. "It's the gas. There must be a leak."

"We need to get everyone out," Miss Thompson said.

"I'll tend to Mrs. Cotton and her cat," Bail said.

No more words were needed. Sue Ann rushed them along, then turned to look up the steps. "Frank, make sure Mr. Brubeck is awake. Clear the upstairs. We've got a gas leak."

Frank turned his attention to the flat bird lying motionless at the bottom of its cage.

Then he bit his bottom lip and pressed his thumb down on the pipe bowl in his pocket.

"I'll see to Brubeck," he said.

Once Frank had the old man safely outside the house with the others, he helped Sue Ann make a head count. The two-story Meeks mansion hovered over the fresh quilt of snow, so recently warm and friendly, now dark and secretive.

The March air was frigid if not below zero, and Bail had his arms wrapped shamelessly around Miss Thompson. The would-be ingenue shivered and stamped her feet.

A husky policeman with a thick mustache approached Sue Ann. "Are all your guests accounted for, Miss Meeks? Is everybody safe?"

Sue Ann said, "Frank?"

Frank assured them both. "Mr. Brubeck is over there beside the elm tree, and you can see Bail and Miss Thompson."

"Mrs. Cotton and her cat are there next to Bail," Sue Ann said.

The officer said, "You say it's a gas leak?"

"Apparently, yes."

His voice was strong and confident. "Let me do a run-through and check it out. Won't be but a moment."

Frank watched as the police officer approached the house, threw open the door, and, covering his mouth and nose with a white handkerchief, ducked inside. Once inside, Frank saw the cop work his way around the perimeter of the house, lifting open windows. Frank put a reassuring hand on Sue Ann's arm. "All's well, Sue. Don't fret."

He'd known her for almost thirty years.

Since the end of the war.

Frank stayed at the house whenever he was in town.

"It's going to be okay. At least the house didn't blow up."

"All clear," the cop said as he trudged back out through the snow. He waved back toward the open door and windows. "I've turned off the gas and got her airing out. By the time you get back inside, it should be clear enough to shut the windows."

"But we can't go back in there, now," Bail said. "We'll freeze to death."

"Some of us will, anyway," Frank said.

"We'll fire up the old woodstove," Sue Ann told them. "And there'll be no charge for the night's stay."

Bail grumbled, and Miss Thompson gently patted his arm in sympathy before she turned to go back inside.

Frank couldn't help but notice a gleam of moonlight along a silver braided ring on her finger. In the other arm, she carried two skeins of blue yarn.

All of them passed the night together in the kitchen around the woodstove.

The next morning as Sue Ellen prepared breakfast, she announced her silver coffee set had been taken from the boardinghouse cabinet. "Along with a set of silver napkin rings and three silver candlestick holders."

The guests gathered once more in the sitting room on the red Persian rug.

"Apparently we've been the target of a crime," Sue Ann said. "Especially heinous considering the timing."

"I don't understand," Bail said. Once more, he sat in the rocker he had claimed for himself during his stay, carving on his wooden finch. Again, Miss Thompson sat on the couch across from him, her yarn-filled basket setting at her feet. Frank stood beside Sue Ann and Mr. Brubeck, allowing gray-haired Mrs. Cotton and her cat to sit in the comfortable chair. The room smelled of woodsmoke, coffee, and tea.

Nary a whiff of gas.

"Somebody took advantage of our misfortune. The silver was stolen while we were clearing the house."

Bail snapped his fingers. "The policeman."

"Surely not," Sue Ann said. "He hardly had the time."

"But who else? We were all accounted for outside." Bail turned to Frank. "You saw it. All of us were there."

Frank tapped his fingers on his chin. "All of us," he said. "Yes, indeed."

Miss Thompson said, "It must've been the policeman."

Sue Ann said, "But how? How could he hide that many items? He wasn't inside that long, and when he came back outside, it wasn't like he was carrying a sack."

"Or wicker basket," Frank said, staring at Miss Thompson.

"I beg your pardon, sir?"

Frank told Sue Ann, "The policeman didn't take your silver. Your guests did."

Miss Thompson cried out. "Frank, you've gone positively mad."

"See here, old man," Bail said.

Sue Ann's voice was skeptical, but calm. "You really must explain yourself, Frank."

He cleared his throat and addressed the group. "Taken one by one, the things I've observed mean nothing. Added together, it indicts all of you."

"Not me," Brubeck said. "I was sleeping like a baby."

Frank shook his head. "Except I don't think you were. I've stayed next door to you for a week. Due to my time in the war, I don't sleep well. I happen to know, you snore every night, all night long. Last night, you didn't make a peep."

"Coffee kept me awake."

"You didn't have any coffee," Frank said. "And speaking of peeps." He addressed Mr. Bail. "Your excuse for waking us was, as you said, life or death."

"Because there was a gas leak."

Frank disagreed. "There was not."

"There was," said Miss Thompson. "Didn't you see the dead bird in the bottom of the cage as you walked by on your way out of the house last night?"

Frank reached into the side pocket of his trousers and took out the carved shape of a finch, painted in lifelike colors of yellow and black. "This bird? It's certainly lifeless. But a skilled rendition, Mr. Bail." Frank said, "Don't pretend it's not your work."

"Certainly it's my work, but where did you find it?"

"Laying on the bottom of the birdcage."

"Nonsense."

"Are you calling me a liar?"

Frank hadn't used such a tone in years, and Bail backed down. "Well, no . . . it's just . . ." He swallowed hard. "If the wooden bird was inside the cage, where's the real bird?"

Frank smiled at Mrs. Cotton. "I'm assuming you fed it to the cat after you made the switch."

The old lady let her jaw drop. "My tabby?"

Frank said, "Mr. Bail was awfully eager to help you out last night. I figure he grabbed the live finch after he dropped in the carving. But he needed to get rid of the bird before it made any noise."

"He fed it to the cat?" Miss Thompson laughed. "Oh, Frank, like I said, you're mad."

Sue Ann knit her eyebrows together. "But there was a gas leak, wasn't there?"

Frank reached into his opposite pants pocket and removed his pipe. He held it up for all to see. "I sat up smoking in my room for more than an hour last night. If there had been a leak, I wouldn't be here. In my experience, neither would the house be here . . . nor any of us."

As Frank explained himself, Miss Thompson's needles had increased their activity. A steady, rhythmic pace had given way to a frantic click, click, click. "What's my place in your lunatic theory, Frank?"

"Bag man."

"Excuse me?"

"Well, bag woman, if you insist," Frank said, tapping her basket with his foot. "If you're leaving in a hurry because of a gas leak, why would you carry two hefty skeins of yarn outside with you last night. My guess is you needed to make room in your basket."

"For all the stolen silver?"

"Exactly."

The needles flashed along. Impossibly fast. "And how did the silver get there?"

"Now we're back to our friendly policeman again."

"Naturally, he's in on the caper. Since everyone except Frank is involved."

"No, naturally since he wears a silver braided wedding ring."

"Does he?"

"I noticed it when he put his hand on Sue Ann's arm."

"Did you?"

"It matches the ring you wear on your finger, Miss Thompson. Or, should I say, Mrs. Thompson?"

The sound from the lady's knitting needles stopped abruptly and she threw them into her knitting basket. "I will not sit here and be accused of common thievery."

Calmly Sue Ann pulled her hand from a long, slit pocket in the side of her skirt, and in it she held a small Derringer pistol. "I think you'll do just that," she said. She waved the gun. "Let's go to your room and see what we might find."

Miss Thompson stamped her feet, but Bail sighed. "Just give back the silver, Doris."

After Doris Thompson gave up her crooked husband and the entire gang was hauled off to jail through the snow, Frank drank fresh coffee with Sue Ann in the sitting room.

"Yours isn't the first house they've hit," he said. "According to the constable, they've tried this trick before."

Sue Ann made a sour face. "I don't like to assume every guest here in my home is a criminal, but I certainly feel foolish falling for their scheme."

"We're all fools now and again. I should know. Spent a big chunk of my life foolish."

"You've done your best to make amends."

"Won't never be enough."

They were quiet for a while, Sue Ann watching him. Finally, she said, "You miss him, don't you? Your brother, I mean."

"Every day for the past fifteen years." Frank sat back in the chair. "He loved you, Sue Ann. Loved staying here when we were in town."

"And we both loved Jesse. He was always a gentleman."

Frank scoffed. "Sometimes. Other times we were both a couple of outlaws and thieves."

"You can't relive the past, Frank. No one can. The most we can hope for is to make a better future, and you've done that. Today you were my gentleman detective, and I love you for it."

She leaned down and kissed him on the forehead. "Now, how about another cup of coffee?"

ABOUT THE AUTHOR

Richard Prosch grew up planting corn, tending cattle, and riding the Nebraska range in a beat-up pickup and a '74 Camaro.

With his wife he developed licensing style guides for several cartoon properties and worked with Tribune Media Services and the Hallmark Channel. In the 2000s, Richard built a web development studio while winning awards for illustration and writing (including a Spur Award from the Western Writers of America). His work has appeared in novels, numerous anthologies, *True West, Wild West, Roundup,* and *Saddlebag Dispatches* magazines, and online at *Boys' Life.*

Richard lives on a Missouri acreage with his wife, Gina, son, Wyatt, and an odd assortment of barn cats.

Printed in the USA
CPSIA information can be obtained
at www.ICGtesting.com
JSHW080954250224
57954JS00001B/32